FORSAKEN

Mary Rice

Solasta Books

FORSAKEN

By

Mary Rice

Never purchase a book without a cover, because to do so is
to purchase stolen property for which the author and publisher have
not been compensated.

Cover art courtesy of FrinaArt

Solasta Books

Charlotte, North Carolina

Visit the website for more novels by M H Rice, including
more books in the Switch series.
MHRicebooks.com

Dear Dad,

Thank you for believing in me and for giving me your love of adventure. I know you're smiling down from heaven.

Love,

Mary

<u>SWITCH TRILOGY</u>

SWITCH

FORSAKEN

RETURN

<u>Other Books by Mary Rice</u>

<u>THE SECRET OF PROPHET HOUSE</u>

<u>TAPESTRY (COMING SOON!)</u>

"Maybe, when time runs out, we will finally know, and regret the loss of what could have been."
Eleanor Grant

CHAPTER 1

Nova stared at what was left of the coffee mug now scattered in a thousand tiny shards across the kitchen floor. Spellbound, she watched as the pool of roasted Colombian coffee with hazelnut cream slowly soaked into her right shoe, turning the nearly white fabric a golden brown. A ridiculous thought crossed her mind—that now she'd have to pour coffee on the other one so they'd match. The rest of the coffee crept across the wood floor in a spiral pattern. Nova was fascinated that the cup could hold enough liquid to produce such an effect.

Something was wrong, but she felt disconnected, as if she were having an out-of-body experience. If she thought about the coffee, she wouldn't have to remember. She could just contemplate the changing color of her shoe, not thinking about what she'd done.

A single stream of coffee broke away from the circle and wrapped around one of the table legs, like a finger grasping for something to hang on to before being sucked back into the murky pool that continued to grow wider and wider. She should probably do something to stop it, but her feet seemed tethered in place while her ferociously beating heart pumped too much blood to her lungs. If she passed out right there on the kitchen floor, how long would it take for someone to find her? Maybe she'd wake up surrounded by all the people she cared about, like Dorothy in *The Wizard of Oz*. *"It wasn't a dream. It was a place. And you, and you, and you, and YOU were there."* But someone was missing—someone with sandy hair and hazel eyes, who loved horses and video games and never stopped talking.

Nova gulped in air and covered her face with her hands as her thin veil of denial crumbled. She squeezed her eyes shut but couldn't stop the visions that flooded her brain. Pretty soon she was going to start screaming and be unable to stop. She shook her head violently, trying to wake up, all the while knowing it was useless.

Her mother's voice drifted in through the screen door. She was laughing and chattering about meaningless things—the weather, running, the neighbor's hideous new awnings. Things that didn't matter. Who cared about rain, or her new running shoes, or the fact that the Jordans' awnings were royal blue and not the *Winsor* blue they'd ordered?

Nova felt a wave of anger and had to fight the urge to rush outside and yell at her mom. *"Marshall's gone! Don't you care?"* But it would be pointless, because Celeste would have no idea who she was talking about. Her mother wasn't a traveler. She didn't know she'd ever had a son.

Nova closed her eyes and focused. Maybe it was still there, the connection to the place she'd traveled from. She tried to block out everything, but the voices in the yard hammered away at her concentration. As she pressed her hands against her ears, her mind groped desperately in the dark. *Please be there!* she prayed over and over.

Her soaked shoe made a squishing sound as she finally backed away from the pool of coffee and dropped into the closest chair next to the kitchen table. Her heart was still pounding, threatening to explode. Nova willed herself to relax by taking slow, deep breaths. Squeezing her eyes shut, she tried to imagine herself back in the four-poster at Willow Hill, the birds chirping in the garden while a gentle breeze floated in through the open window. Somewhere off in the distance, there would be a lawnmower or tractor running. Aunt Jean had said that you weren't in the country if you couldn't hear a one of those.

As her heart rate slowed, Nova allowed herself the fantasy that she was back at Aunt Jean's. That nothing had happened. She could almost smell her aunt's chocolate pies baking in the double ovens downstairs and hear the horses stomping out in the barn, waiting for their feed bins to be filled. *Everything will be all right if I can just get back there,* she told herself as she searched frantically for the lifeline back to last night, back to Willow Hill.

But there was nothing, not even the thinnest thread. Too much time had passed while she had been reveling in her new reality, convinced she'd made the perfect switch. The connection was gone. Just like Grandma Kate years ago, she was stuck in this timeline—without Marshall. It was possible she'd never see him again. He'd never pester her to play video games or take him to a movie. She'd never patch him up when he fell off his skateboard or wait for him at the bus stop or tell him to shut up when he talked on and on about something only a nine-year-old would care about. All the little things that had bothered her now seemed so trivial, even endearing. She'd give anything to go back to last night, gliding back and forth on the porch swing while Marshall jabbered on and on about the horses.

"Justin said I'm the fastest learner he's ever seen! He said Bo can be my horse any time I'm down here! Nobody else can ride him! It'll be like he's really mine, won't it?"

Nova had barely paid any attention to his constant chattering. She'd been relieved when the motion of the swing had finally knocked him out. All she'd been able to think about was her dead sister. There'd been no room to consider anyone else.

Nova pictured Marshall sleeping beside her on the swing, bits of hay sticking out of his hair. *I did this. I killed my brother,* she thought bitterly. Marshall had been alive not even twenty-four hours ago. How could he be dead? No, not dead. *Erased.* Nova's eyes flew open as a Mount St. Helens-sized adrenaline rush hit her. Exploding out of the chair, she bolted down the hallway and yanked on the office door that used to lead to Marshall's room. Locked! She pounded on the door, unconcerned that anyone in the house could hear her. What difference did it make? Who cared if they thought she was crazy? She had no intention of staying here without her little brother. Nothing else mattered but finding a way back and undoing her mistake, because a reality without Marshall was unthinkable.

"Dad! Open the door!"

Nova paused and listened, trying to catch her breath. There was no sound, but he had to be in there. She dashed into her room and dropped to the floor beside her bed, praying that the Nova in this reality had also hidden a key to the office. Sure enough, it was taped to the frame just like before.

Racing back, Nova jammed the key in the lock and jerked open the door. Her dad was sitting at the desk with his head in his hands, rocking back and forth. His bowl of mints lay shattered on the floor next to the door. Books and papers were strewn about as if a huge gust of wind had come up suddenly, slinging around everything that wasn't bolted down. Except the huge wind had been Dayton Grant.

"Dad—" Nova broke down, sobbing. How could she not have seen this possibility? *Stupid!*

"Oh my God, Nova. He's gone. Marshall's gone."

She took a deep breath and tried to pull herself together, hastily wiping her eyes with the back of her hand. "I have to fix this. We can't stay here."

Dayton's palm was bleeding. Nova dashed out of the room and came back moments later with a hand towel. She gently wrapped it around his hand and laid her head on his shoulder.

"I'm so sorry. I shouldn't have tried to get Alana back on my own." He continued to rock, ignoring her comment until she grabbed him by the shoulders and shook him. "I'm gonna get him back."

The truth was she didn't know how she'd done what she'd done in the first place. She'd been reckless, not fully understanding or respecting the power she was playing with, and she'd made a tragic mess of everything.

Nova thought of the painting in the attic at Aunt Jean's—Grandma Kate's family that no longer existed. Would someone find a painting of Marshall in a trunk years from now and wonder about the little boy with sandy hair and hazel eyes?

"We just went camping last weekend." Dayton looked at her, his eyes glazed over.

"This is my fault—" She struggled to catch her breath.

Dayton shook his head. "I can't blame you. The truth is I wanted you to travel. When we talked in the garden… I hoped you'd do it. You're stronger than I am. I figured, with Aunt Jean helping you… I don't know. It just seemed possible that everything would work out. I'd have all three of my kids together finally." He looked down at the towel. A tiny spot of blood had made it through.

"Dad, what are we going to do?"

He took a couple of ragged breaths before looking at her. "I think the worst thing we can do is panic and try to travel again on our own. We need help."

"We need Aunt Jean," Nova said firmly, shaking off her growing despair. "She'll know what to do."

"Aunt Jean!" Dayton's face turned red and he slammed his other fist on the desk, causing the last few papers that were hanging precariously along the edge to fall off. "If we hadn't gone to see her, none of this would've happened! Marshall would still be here!"

"But Alana would still be dead. Look, I messed things up, not Aunt Jean. She didn't tell me to go ahead and travel. I decided on my own."

His anger dissipated, and he sat back in his chair. "I guess I know that. It's just easier to blame her. If I'd been stronger years ago, there wouldn't have been a need for you to take matters into your own hands."

"Okay. I screwed up. You screwed up. It's done. All that matters now is changing timelines again to one that includes Marshall. And we have to keep our heads straight. Mom and Alana can't know about any of this. We have to be as normal as possible until we figure things out."

"*Normal*," he repeated, sounding like someone who'd just woken from a deep sleep. "Right. I guess we need to think about some damage control." He seemed to be slipping away into his own thoughts. "If anyone else was home, they'd have been in here by now, wanting to know what all the ruckus was. We must be alone." He stared at the mess he'd made. "I don't remember doing this."

"We better clean it up. This'll be hard to explain."

"Yeah."

Nova lowered her voice. "I know Mom went for a run, but where's Alana?" Dayton didn't seem to hear her, so Nova shook him again, gently. "Where's Alana?"

He looked up. "She left with what's-his-name. David? I don't know where they went."

"Good." Nova felt a wave of relief. "You clean up. I'm calling Aunt Jean. She'll help us." Nova grabbed the desk phone off of the cradle. "I need Aunt Jean's number."

Her dad was still looking around the room at the wreck he'd created. "This will take forever to clean it up."

"Dad! Her number?"

He pulled a small address book from the top drawer of the desk and handed it to Nova, then he began to pick up papers from the floor and place them on the desk, one by one. Feeling a pain in the pit of her stomach, she watched for a moment as he moved around the office. What if there was nothing they could do? The only hope was Aunt Jean. She was the only person who could possibly know how to get Marshall back. Maybe she'd come up here and take over, make things right again.

Nova started to dial her aunt's number on the desk phone but hesitated, thinking it would be better if she called from her room. Her dad's shuffling around the office was making her so keyed up that she felt as though she was on the verge of losing it again.

"I'll be back," she said. "Stay here, okay?"

He didn't answer but continued his effort to put the room back in order.

Nova paused at the office door, looking back at him. "I can't do this by myself," she said quietly.

He looked up. "I know, firefly. I'll be okay." He turned his attention back to the trashed room. "I hope you're right about Aunt Jean. I'd hate to be stuck here." He sounded resigned, as if he'd already accepted that nothing could be done.

"We're not staying here," Nova stated firmly.

She retreated quickly to her room, closed the door, and flipped through the book until she found what she was looking for. Picking up the phone on her nightstand, she dialed Willow Hill and waited.

It rang at least a dozen times before a strange male voice answered. "Hello?"

Nova was taken aback. It didn't sound like Justin, but what other man would be answering Aunt Jean's phone? "This is Nova."

"Hi, Nova. It's Michael."

"Michael?" She struggled to place him.

"Sorry I haven't called. I just got back here two days ago. I had to fly home for a couple of weeks after the funeral. Minor catastrophe at work that needed my attention. I was planning to call your dad in the morning to let him know it's taking a little longer than I expected to go through Aunt Jean's investments. I had no idea she had so many. It's impressive. Plus, I don't think she or my parents ever threw anything away." He chuckled, sounding more weary than amused. "The attic alone is a nightmare. I opened one of the trunks and it was stuffed with dolls. There must have been fifteen or twenty. I almost passed out."

Nova was stricken, unable to respond.

"Nova, you there?"

"Yes," she said quietly. "The dolls were Georgia's."

"Really? They were Mom's? I don't remember her collecting dolls, but I've been out of the house since college," Michael said. "I guess Aunt Jean kept them for sentimental reasons."

"I think so." Nova heard herself responding, but she felt no connection to the voice.

"Well, I ended up leaving the attic alone. Except for a few things she knew I wanted, she left the house and everything in it to your dad. So he can deal with it whenever he's ready. I'm happy I don't have to."

"Okay," Nova responded, barely able to process what he was saying.

"Give me until tomorrow. Then I'll call Dayton and we'll figure everything out. I think he'll need to come back down here though. It's going to be tedious going through all the paperwork, but we have some decisions to make. Hold on—" She heard someone talking in the background. "The attorney's here, so I need to run. Can you give your dad the message?"

"Sure," she managed.

Nova placed the phone back on the stand and stared at it as the words swirled around inside her head, over and over, as if they were actually being spoken aloud. *Aunt Jean is dead.*

CHAPTER 2

The bedroom door cracked open and Dayton stuck his head in. "Did you call her?" Nova's stricken expression must have spoken volumes because all of the color drained from his face. "What's wrong? What did she say?"

Nova toyed with the idea of stalling, keeping him in the dark for just a little while. He seemed fragile, ready to break apart at any moment. How could she tell him that the only person they knew who could help get Marshall back was gone? Aunt Jean was the rock of the family, bigger than life. She made anything seem possible. And she was the only one who knew about traveling.

Nova hesitated before taking a deep breath and plunging in. Better to get it over with. He'd learn the truth sooner or later anyway. "I didn't talk to her."

"You didn't?" He seemed confused. "Let's do it now then. We can call from the office."

"I already called Willow Hill."

"You called? But you said you didn't."

"No, I said I didn't talk to her."

"Okay, so you called," he responded, irritation seeping into his voice. "What happened? Why didn't you talk to her?"

"Michael answered."

"Michael?" Dayton frowned. "Uncle Bill's son Michael?"

"Yeah. He was there because… he was taking inventory of Aunt Jean's possessions."

"Why was Michael—" Dayton closed his eyes, suddenly aware. When he opened them again, he had a vacant look. "She's dead too, isn't she? Like Marshall."

"Marshall isn't dead."

"You know what I mean!" Dayton said angrily. "He's not alive. And now Aunt Jean is dead." He closed the door and leaned against it, shaking his head. "What happened?"

"I don't know. He didn't say."

"She was so healthy… alive. What could've possibly changed in this timeline?"

Nova felt sure that it had been Aunt Jean who had come into her room at Willow Hill and touched her face, telling her to "let go." Was that why she had died? But that was in a different timeline. It didn't make sense.

"Do you think she died because she helped me? Do you think that did something to her? She said the power gets weaker the more you travel. Maybe the person gets weaker too."

Dayton sat on the bed beside Nova. "If Aunt Jean helped you, that was her choice. She must have had a reason. She knew better than anyone what the repercussions would be. And we don't know that that had anything to do with her dying in this timeline."

"I wish I could ask her." Nova felt tears spilling down her cheeks. She wiped them away with the back of her hand.

"Yeah…"

"We'll find someone to help us, right?" Nova asked hopefully.

Dayton's tone changed to one of despair as he shook his head sadly. "There's no one left."

"There are other Grants, aren't there? We can't be the only ones left. There must be more family somewhere."

He wasn't listening. "I can't believe this is happening." He moaned. "I didn't realize… all morning.

How is that possible? I didn't even think about him at first. He was gone and I didn't even notice."

"I know. Me too. I was so focused on Alana that it didn't hit me right away about Marshall."

"Yesterday I promised him we'd go camping again in a couple of weeks." Dayton's voice broke. "Now I may never see him again."

"We'll see him." Nova wished she could just lose it like her dad. She felt as if someone had ripped away a piece of her. She wanted to scream and crawl in a hole, let someone else fix this. But there wasn't anyone else.

Dayton sat on her bed while Nova paced. Marshall didn't exist in this new timeline. He'd never existed. So they couldn't go back in time to change anything. Going forward wouldn't do any good either for the same reason. *There has to be a way.*

"There must be other family." Nova frowned. "What about Michael? He's Uncle Bill's son. Wouldn't he be a traveler too? And if he is, he'd know more about it than we do."

Dayton thought about that for a minute, then shook his head. "Not everyone has the gift. I remember Aunt Jean talking about it when I was at her house when I was a kid. She said her nephew wasn't a traveler so I shouldn't talk to him about it. Of course, he was a kid too, so who knows. I remember Uncle Bill saying some are late bloomers. Maybe he was disappointed his own son couldn't travel though and it was just wishful thinking."

"Still, it's worth trying to find out."

"Sure, I guess," he agreed halfheartedly.

The phone on Nova's nightstand rang, and they both nearly jumped out of their skin then stared at it wide-eyed, as if ringing was the most unnatural thing a phone could do.

There were two phone lines into the house—the main line and Nova's private line. Delilah was the only other teenager Nova knew with a private line. It made clandestine late-night phone calls a lot easier. But it was the main line ringing, not hers.

"We should answer it," Nova said quietly, making no attempt to do that. "It could be Mom or Alana."

Dayton didn't move. After seven or eight rings, the answering machine in the office picked up. Even through the closed door, Nova could make out a woman's voice. She glanced at Dayton, who was sitting in stunned silence, his face as white as a sheet. Nova got up and opened the door so they could hear more clearly.

"...and it would be nice to finally see your children again, but I'm afraid I just can't. It's a long drive and I haven't been feeling well since Jean died. I'm sorry I didn't get down there for the funeral. Too many memories, I suppose. Thank you for sending me the pictures. Well, give my love to Celeste and the girls. I'd love to talk to you, son. Call me when you can."

Dayton jumped up and hurried into the office as the recording finished. He stood over the answering machine, staring at it as if he expected the caller to burst out any minute.

"Dad? Who was that?"

He looked up with a stunned expression. "My mother."

"Grandma Kate? She's been dead for almost ten years"

Even as she said it, she knew it didn't matter. Anything could change when you switched timelines.

"I guess she's not dead anymore," he said quietly, collapsing into his desk chair. "Oh my God…"

Nova felt a flicker of hope. Maybe their situation wasn't as dire as they'd thought it was. "This is great news! She's Aunt Jean's sister. She knows about traveling. She'll help us figure out what to do about Marshall."

Her dad clearly didn't feel as hopeful. "She hates traveling. She won't even talk about it."

"Maybe she's different now. You don't know how

she'll feel in this timeline. What did she mean about finally seeing us again? Why wouldn't we have seen her?"

"I don't know. Mother and I never really got along that well. I mean, she loved me of course, but there was always tension between us. She was overprotective and never wanted me to go anywhere or try anything she thought was *risky*, which pretty much covered everything. I thought she'd never even let me get a driver's license. I had to threaten to quit school."

Nova thought about Grandma Kate's first family. Losing them had apparently made her paranoid. But her dad didn't know about Daniel and the baby. Maybe telling him would make him feel differently about his mother. "Dad, Aunt Jean told me something when we were at Willow Hill. It was the morning I practiced traveling."

"What did she tell you?" He frowned, obviously worried about hearing more bad news.

Nova took a deep breath. "Did you know about Grandma Kate's first husband?"

He seemed taken aback. "She was married before my father?"

"Yes. She married a man named Daniel. Grandma Kate and Aunt Jean were living with their parents, your grandparents, and he bought the house next door to fix up and sell. Anyway, Kate and Daniel fell in love against your grandparents' wishes and got married. They moved into the house next door instead of selling it, and I guess a year or so later, they had a baby boy named Danny Jr." Nova paused to let her dad take it in. His expression was unreadable, so she continued. "Having the baby patched things up with the family. Everybody loved him. He'd follow Daniel around with a toy hammer, pretending to help him fix things. Aunt Jean painted a picture of them on the porch."

Dayton was thunderstruck. "There's a picture of them? Where?"

"At Willow Hill, in the attic. I found it when I was up there looking around."

"You found a picture of my mother with another family and you didn't tell me?"

"I didn't know who they were at the time. I found out later, when I was talking to Aunt Jean."

"And you still didn't tell me?"

"I'm sorry! Can we get past this? I'm telling you now. Besides, I thought Aunt Jean would tell you."

"Is there anything else you haven't told me?" he asked flatly.

"No." Nova shook her head solemnly.

Dayton stared off into space for a moment. "What happened to them, my mother's other family?"

Nova collected her thoughts. "Daniel was working on the roof, and he fell off and broke his neck. A few days later, Grandma Kate tried to travel back to the morning of the accident to stop him. But when she traveled, her mind wandered because she was still too upset to focus. She ended up going back too far. Instead of traveling back a few days, she traveled back four years."

"Why four years?" Dayton asked.

"She was thinking about their house. There'd been a fire there years before, and I guess that crossed her mind just before she traveled. She went back to the night of the fire. When she did, it changed everything. She waited a year for the day she'd meet Daniel, but he never came. Aunt Jean said Kate sat on their front porch for weeks, waiting for him. They all wanted to help her, but she wouldn't let them."

"She never saw him again?" Dayton's voice was without expression. He sounded numb.

"No. She never found out what happened to him. So of course, she never had the baby either. That's why she hated traveling. That's why she was overprotective of you. She didn't want to lose you too."

Dayton sat back in his chair and stared at Nova for a couple of minutes, obviously trying to come to terms with this new information. Then he leaned forward. "That's an awful secret to carry around. Why didn't she ever tell me?"

"I don't know. Maybe she didn't want to make you feel like second place or something."

"Yeah, maybe. So if she had been successful, you and I wouldn't even be here."

"I guess not."

"This explains a lot. I guess I can't blame her for deciding not to travel again. Maybe if she'd known about going forward like we did, that would have made a difference. But then, like I said, we wouldn't be here."

"Your grandparents finally sent her to stay with relatives in Charleston."

"That's where she met my dad," he said solemnly. "I don't know who those relatives were. Mother never really talked about them, but I remember they had a different last name."

"Aunt Jean didn't say how they were related," Nova said. "There's something else she told me. She said Grandma Kate could have gone back to the day she traveled from but she waited too long."

"What do you mean?"

"When we were in the garden talking to Aunt Jean, do you remember her telling us about hopping back in time briefly and returning to where we started?"

Dayton shook his head. "Not really. I was trying to make sense of everything she said. I guess that information didn't stick."

"Well, when you travel, you can go right back to where you started if you don't wait too long. I don't know how much time you have, maybe just minutes. There's a connection that lasts a short while and then it's gone. She said you can feel it."

Dayton leaned forward in his chair. "I never felt anything when I traveled. Did you?"

Nova shook her head. "No, but I wasn't looking for it. I guess I'd forgotten there even *was* a connection. When I got here, I thought everything was perfect and I was so happy to see Alana that I wasn't looking for a way back. When I realized Marshall wasn't here, I tried to find it. I don't know what it's supposed to feel like, but there was nothing there."

"I think I'm finally starting to realize how complicated and risky this traveling thing is. Switching timelines isn't something you should ever jump into lightly. It's a wonder anyone manages to do it without screwing everything up. Why didn't we see that before? My mother always said how dangerous this gift was and no one believed her. Now I think she may be the only sane person in the family," he said sadly.

"We didn't know this would happen. Now it doesn't matter," she said frankly. "All that matters is finding a way to change to another timeline that has everyone in it, including Marshall. That's all I care about."

"We'll talk to my mother, but I honestly don't know what she'll be able or willing to do. She turned from the family years ago." He frowned. "She wouldn't even talk to her own sister, though I know she missed her."

"But she grew up around travelers. Her whole family had the gift. If we tell her what's at stake, she'll have to help! We're talking about her grandson!"

"You don't know her, Nova. She's stubborn. Traveling doesn't change who you are—your temperament or personality. You're still you. My mother is still the same person, and once she decides something, that's it."

"Let me talk to her." Nova was determined. "I'll make her understand."

"You can try. It's not like we really have a choice."

The back door slammed and Alana came flitting down the hall, sticking her head in the office door. "What's up with you two? You're not ready and you look like you just ran over the dog." Alana waited for an answer while Dayton and Nova exchanged looks.

"We don't have a dog," Nova finally replied, forcing a smile.

"Well that's a relief." Alana laughed. "Holy crap!

What happened to your office? Dad, are you bleeding?"

"It's just a paper cut, and the office… I was having, I mean… acting out this thing for a book. Forget it. Doesn't matter." Dayton was completely flustered. They'd have to come up with a better story before Celeste showed up.

"Mom's gonna freak," Alana declared. "I'm getting out of here." She disappeared for a second, then stuck her head back in the door again. "Better get ready, little sister. David *and Ethan* will be here soon!"

"Wait—what? Ethan's coming to dinner with us?" Nova felt a panic attack revving up, her heart suddenly threatening to leap out of her chest. Trying to seem normal with the family would be hard enough. If Ethan was along, it would be impossible!

"I invited him. I knew you wouldn't mind." Alana winked and took off up the hall to her room.

When they heard her door close, Nova turned to Dayton. "Dad…"

"I know. I forgot about the party."

CHAPTER 3

Nova stepped out of the shower onto the cool tile floor and shivered. Wrapping herself in a towel, she stood in front of the mirror and watched the condensation evaporate, gradually revealing her reflection. Internally, she felt as if she'd been chewed up in a meat grinder, but externally, she looked utterly normal. She'd traveled through time, changed her reality, brought her sister back from the dead, and obliterated her little brother. How could so much change and not leave a mark?

Just let me get through tonight, she prayed. *Then we'll set things right and it won't matter.*

A trickle of water ran down Nova's back from her soaking wet hair, making her shiver harder. She took a deep breath and pulled the towel snuggly around her before stepping out of the bathroom and down the hall to her room. If Marshall were alive, he'd be banging on her door about now, demanding that she hurry up. Marshall loved parties. Actually, Marshall loved just about everything. Nova tried to imagine herself yanking open her bedroom door and surprising him. She could hear his peals of laughter as he took off up the hall. How many times had she chased him, yelling at him to quit bothering her while she was in her room with the door shut. He'd invariably make that pitiful face and she'd cave.

Nova tried to imagine that look he'd given her a hundred times, but for some reason, she couldn't picture it.

As a matter of fact, she couldn't picture his face at all. Slightly alarmed, she tried harder to see his image but still wasn't able to summon it. She could imagine his hair, his eyes, his smile, even the way he dressed, but couldn't put it all together to form a clear picture of her little brother. Was this reality blotting him out? Was that why Aunt Jean had painted Kate's family? So she wouldn't forget what they looked like?

Nova felt panic setting in. It hadn't even been twenty-four hours! She concentrated, willing his image to appear, straining to put together the pieces of Marshall like a jigsaw puzzle. And then finally, there he was—unruly hair, quirky smile, and all. Nova dropped to the floor and wept.

"Thank God. Thank God," she muttered over and over. *Don't worry, kiddo. I won't forget, and I'm coming back for you.*

Nearly an hour later, Nova emerged, wearing a pale green top, black skirt, and sandals. Her hair fell in soft, natural waves down her back. She paused to look at her reflection again, this time in the full-length mirror by her bedroom door. Still normal. No one would suspect that she didn't belong here or that she was sick with grief because this reality was missing a little boy who bore a striking resemblance to her formerly dead sister.

She tiptoed to her dad's office and let herself in. Dayton was sitting at his desk, a somber expression on his face. He looked up when Nova entered the room.

"Hi, firefly," he said quietly before turning his attention back to the sketch in front of him.

"What are you drawing?" Nova asked, shutting the door.

"Marshall. I don't want to forget him."

Nova felt her heart jump into her throat. So he'd noticed it too? How hard it was to picture Marshall? She walked around and looked over his shoulder. Her eyes filled with tears as she gazed at the face of her little brother. Her dad had captured him perfectly—his unruly hair, the way his mouth turned up slightly at the corners. Marshall gazed up from the page, his hazel eyes full of mischief.

"That's perfect," she said.

"I felt like I was forgetting him, like he was fading away or something. But then I started drawing and he came back to me."

"It's him." Nova wrapped her arms around her dad. "You did good."

"Thanks, honey." He continued to stare at the drawing. "That's what happened before… with your sister. That's why I drew her over and over. Sometimes I'd lie in bed and try to picture her face and I couldn't. So I'd come in here and look at the sketches and she'd come back to me."

"I know."

"You noticed it too?" He looked at her.

"Yeah," she answered, wiping her eyes to keep them from spilling over. This wallowing in remorse was getting them nowhere. Nova set her jaw and put her hand on her dad's arm to stop him. "Come on. You have to get ready."

Dayton frowned. "Why? What difference does it make? We're not staying here, so why do we need to bother pretending?"

"We agreed. We have to keep things normal," Nova pointed out even though he had agreed to nothing. Nova needed everything to be as normal and steady as possible. That was the only way she'd be able to keep from losing it. "Dad, I'm freaked out too, but if everything around here gets crazy and Mom and Alana start asking a bunch of questions, we won't be able to focus enough to figure out what to do."

"Okay." He began to work on his drawing again, lovingly adding details to his sketch.

How many pictures would there be of her little brother in that file after sixteen years? Would Alana find them all someday and wonder who he was? Nova felt herself slipping into despair again but shook it off.

She leaned in close to her dad and said with a confidence she didn't really feel, "I somehow managed to bring Alana back after she'd been dead for sixteen years. Marshall's been gone a day. I can do it."

"That's another thing we have to talk about."

"What do you mean?" Nova asked, but she knew exactly what he was saying.

"What about Alana? What if bringing Marshall back, if that's even possible, means we have to give up Alana? What if she can't be alive in a reality that includes him? Your mom and I wanted two kids. When Alana… well… after a while, we decided to try again. That's when we had Marshall. If Alana had lived, we probably wouldn't have had any more children. So what if we have to repeat history in order to get your brother back? And how would we even do that?" Dayton looked at his sketch. "I want my son back more than anything, but I can't lose Alana again. We have to figure out a way to have them both. I can't bear the thought of having to choose."

"I know." Nova felt the weight of their situation bearing down on her, but she gathered herself up. "I don't care what it takes. We'll find a way to have them both."

She hoped it was true, but doubt had wrapped itself around her heart, infecting every feeling, every thought, like a weed sucking the life out of a once-vibrant flower. Deep down, a reality that would never include her brother seemed more and more inevitable. *Never existed.* How would they manage to get around that?

Oblivious to Nova's internal battle, Dayton brightened a little. "You're right, firefly." He stood and put his arms around her. "Be patient with your old man. We'll bring Marshall back somehow and everything will be like it was, except we'll have Alana too."

Nova nodded. "Right. We'll have Alana too."

She hoped she sounded more certain than she felt. Truth be known, she had developed the ability to lie at the drop of a hat. But a lie *felt* different than the truth. The truth didn't leave a bitter taste behind. It didn't give her a sinking feeling in the pit of her stomach. Her comment didn't feel like the truth.

The office door cracked opened, and Celeste poked her head in. "Really, Day? That's what you're planning to wear? Oh my—! What happened in here?"

"Sorry, honey. Just give me a few minutes to clean this up and change clothes." He managed a weak smile.

"Day, what on earth?"

"I was… um… having a writer's block moment. I thought trashing the place, acting out a scene, would help clear my head." Dayton was the worst liar Nova had ever heard. There was no way that explanation would fly with her mom.

Celeste stood there frowning. "You aren't getting sick, are you?"

"No, babe, I'm fine. Ten minutes. That's all I need." This time he managed a believable smile.

Celeste shook her head and turned her attention to Nova. "Did you make that mess in the kitchen?"

"What mess?" Nova had no idea what she was talking about.

"Your dad's coffee cup, or what's left of it, was in pieces on the floor and coffee was everywhere! What's going on around here today? First that mess and now this one!"

Nova had completely forgotten about dropping the cup earlier. "I'm sorry, Mom. I'll clean up the kitchen."

"Never mind, I took care of it."

"Sorry about that." Nova forced a smile.

"I'll cut you some slack because it's your birthday." Celeste smiled. "Come on. Let your dad get ready. We have a surprise for you at the party." She winked at Dayton and ducked out, but not before giving the room another sweep with her eyes, followed by a loud sigh.

"I don't know about you, Dad, but I can't handle any more surprises," Nova whispered. "Any idea what she's talking about?"

"Nope. Just go with it, honey. Whatever it is won't

matter when we switch again."

A moment later, they heard Celeste knocking on Alana's bedroom door, urging her to hurry up. Dayton pulled himself together and headed off to change clothes while Nova stood over the desk, still looking at Marshall's picture. It had seemed like a perfect likeness, but now something about it looked wrong. She couldn't put her finger on it, but it bothered her. She picked up the sketch and examined it, determined to find the mistake. Her dad had captured his features perfectly. She was sure of that. But there was definitely something *off*.

Alana burst into the room again and grabbed the drawing out of Nova's hand. "What's this? Another one of Dad's book people?" She handed the picture back to Nova.

"Book people?"

"Yeah. You know, the characters he dreams up for his books." Alana laughed.

"Oh, yeah," Nova answered, though she didn't remember ever referring to the characters in her dad's books as "book people." Of course, that was probably because Alana had made up the term and she was dead in the last timeline. *Maybe I should tell you that. Maybe I should tell you that you've only been alive for a day...*

A chill ran up Nova's spine as she suddenly realized what was wrong with Marshall's picture. Her dad had drawn a faint dimple in his left cheek. But Marshall didn't have a dimple. Alana did.

"Nova! What's wrong with you?"

"What?"

"You looked like you were having one of those absence seizures, like that kid down the street. What's the deal with that picture?"

"I don't know. It looks like you, don't you think?"

Nova held up the drawing, and Alana studied it for a moment.

"Well, that's a little creepy. I guess I just have one of those faces that begs to be copied." She laughed.

"I guess so," Nova mumbled. She placed the sketch back on the desk and started to follow her sister out of the office, but then turned back.

"Come on!" Alana sounded impatient.

"I'll be there in a sec. I just have to do something." Nova sat in her dad's chair and studied the picture.

"Oh my God. You're just like Dad," Alana said as she flitted out the door and up the hallway.

Nova picked up the pencil and flipped it over before carefully erasing the dimple. When she was finished, she sat back and studied the image again, smiling. *There you are, kiddo.*

"Nova!" Celeste called.

"Coming." Nova jumped up.

Her mother was at the front door, loaded down with packages. "Where's your dad? I need help getting these to the car."

"He's getting ready," Nova reminded her as Alana walked in. "We can help you."

"You're not carrying your own gifts to the car." Celeste turned and looked toward the driveway. "Here comes David." She smiled approvingly.

David strode up the sidewalk with an obvious confidence that said he'd been there many times. "I can help you with that, Mrs. Grant."

"David! Thank goodness. I don't know what's taking Dayton so long." Celeste handed the packages to David. He looked back over his shoulder at a smiling Alana.

"Isn't my boyfriend hot?" Alana whispered. She grabbed her purse and started to follow him but stopped at the doorway. "Looks like Ethan's here too. Nice truck." Alana winked.

Nova ran to the door in time to see Ethan walking up the driveway. It was as if nothing had changed, except for the fact that her deceased sister was standing on the front porch grinning from ear to ear, a thought that made Nova giggle before she could catch herself. She felt her heartbeat quicken and her cheeks go red.

"Jeez. Don't be so obvious!" Alana laughed. "At least make him work for it a little."

Nova jabbed her sister in the side and stepped off the porch. When Ethan walked up, his cheeks were slightly flushed. Nova wondered if he'd heard Alana's remark. If he had, at least he had the decency to be embarrassed.

"I can take you in my truck if that's okay," he offered.

"Sure." Nova blushed again, mentally chastising herself for having so little control over her emotions. Alana was right. She needed to tone down her reaction to him. Her dad was putting packages in the car, but her mom watched them, smiling. Nova waved. "I'm riding with Ethan, okay?"

"Of course!" Celeste answered, obviously pleased.

Ethan stepped aside and gave a slight bow. "After you, birthday girl."

She slid into the familiar seat beside him. If she let herself, she could rest her hand on his arm while he drove, as she had so many times before. Of course, he didn't know that.

When they pulled up to a light, Nova glanced at Ethan. His hair was a little shorter than it had been in the last timeline, but it still fell a little over one of his amazing blue eyes. David was attractive—with his dark hair, athletic build, and chiseled features—but he didn't hold a candle to Ethan. Everything about Ethan took her breath away. Not wanting him to catch her staring, she gazed out the window for a minute. When they stopped at a red light, she looked back and found him watching her, smiling.

"What?" she asked, embarrassed.

"I was just thinking. All the time I stalked you at school, I never expected to be driving you to your sixteenth birthday party."

"Oh." Nova looked down at her hands, not sure how to respond.

"I could get used to this."

"What?"

"Driving you around in my truck."

"Oh." Nova couldn't seem to speak around him. *Is "oh" all I can say? He's going to think there's something wrong with me.* She cleared her throat. "So how long have you had Sam's truck?"

"How do you know Sam?"

Nova felt her heart speed up. *Stupid!* Of course she shouldn't know Sam! Maybe it was better to keep her mouth shut. What was it her mom always said? Better to say nothing and be thought a fool than to open your mouth and prove it.

"Nova?"

"Sorry. I guess you must have said something about him earlier."

Ethan was watching her with a baffled expression. There was an awkward silence as the light changed to green, and they turned from Riverbank onto Settlers Road, finally pulling up to Mario's Italian Restaurant.

"I guess some things don't change," Nova spoke without thinking again.

"What do you mean?" asked Ethan.

"Nothing. We just came—I mean *come* here a lot." Nova reminded herself once again to be more careful about blurting things out.

"You don't seem very excited."

"About what?"

"Your birthday. Turning sixteen."

"Oh. Not as much as I thought I'd be," Nova answered honestly, relieved to be able to say what she was actually thinking.

"Really? Why not?"

"I don't know." She wasn't doing a good job of acting normal, but the stress of guarding her words was wearing on her. She took a deep breath and gave him the best smile she could manage. "But I'm excited about the party."

"Well, that's good!" Ethan took the key out of the ignition and opened his door. Nova reached for her door handle, but Ethan stopped her. "Allow me, princess."

He hopped out and jogged around to her door, then opened it with a flourish. This Ethan was a little more dramatic than the other one. *The other one?* Nova shook her head. *There aren't two Ethans, you idiot!*

CHAPTER 4

Alana and David were already inside the restaurant, and so were about twenty-five other kids their age. Nova's heart jumped into her throat when she realized that, while most of them were familiar, she didn't really know at least half of them and certainly hadn't been friends with them in her other life. This was going to be a nightmare! How could she possibly get through several hours in a room full of people she barely knew who thought they were her friends?

Before she could dwell on her predicament, two girls ran over and grabbed her. They were dressed almost exactly alike, in short denim skirts and cropped tops. Nova wondered if their matching outfits were intentional or if they were just that clueless. She'd seen both girls at school, usually walking down the hall with their heads together, giggling and jabbering away. She tried to summon up their names but couldn't.

"Happy birthday, Nova!" they shouted practically in unison before turning their attention to Ethan. "Are you two dating?"

"Well, that depends." He winked at the ditzy twin on the left.

"He drove me to the party. That's all." Nova shot him a scathing look while the two girls fell into a fit of giggles.

The ditzy twin on the right tossed her blond hair back over her shoulder in a move she obviously thought was alluring. Nova glanced at the other girl, who had wrapped her arm around Ethan's. *They must be friends of Alana's.* She gave Ethan a sideways glare.

The hair-tosser leaned in and whispered in Nova's ear, "So he's still available?"

Nova pulled away, rolling her eyes. "I need to talk to Alana."

She gave Ethan a withering look, but he just grinned, obviously enjoying being the object of so much female attention. Nova made her way through the crowd, reminding herself to smile as the other teens wished her a happy birthday. Oddly enough, she practically ran into Joanna, who looked totally different without a scowl on her face. Delilah was right behind her.

"Great party!" gushed Joanna.

"Thanks," Nova muttered.

"What's up with you and Ethan?" Delilah asked nonchalantly. Her eyes darted over to him as he held an audience with the ditzy twins.

He had one on each arm now, but at least he had the decency to look uncomfortable. Delilah's feeble attempt at sounding disinterested didn't fool Nova. After months of being Delilah's best friend, Nova could tell she was seething internally. She apparently had a crush on him in this timeline too.

"I don't know, Dee. I guess we're dating."

Delilah tore her eyes away from Ethan and looked at Nova, a baffled expression on her face. "Nobody calls me Dee except my mom. And I hate it."

"Sorry," Nova responded, anxious to get away before she said something else wrong. "I need to talk to my sister."

With that, she made a beeline for Alana, who was chattering away on the other side of the room with David standing dutifully at her side. Nova had to give her credit. From the look on her face, Alana was comfortable being the center of attention. She also seemed to genuinely enjoy talking with each of her friends. Nova envied her ease. Social occasions involving lots of people had always been a little awkward for Nova. David seemed to share that sentiment and looked relieved when she came over.

"Finally. Someone to talk to," he whispered, smiling.

"I wasn't really up for a party tonight," Nova admitted.

"Me either. But what can you do?" David grinned. "When you date Alana, every day's a party." He laughed. "But I guess you know that since you live with her."

"Yeah." Nova bit her tongue to keep from blurting out, *Actually, I've only known her for one day, so it's all new to me.*

"Hey," Ethan said softly in her ear, making her jump.

"Ethan! Don't sneak up on me!" Nova's heart was pounding from yet another adrenaline rush. She wondered if one of these times it would just explode.

"Don't be mad about those two. They're idiots. I was just having some fun with them."

"They're not what I'm mad about. What's wrong with you? Why are you so different?" she asked without thinking.

He looked taken aback. "Different than what?"

"Different than… I don't know. Just forget it."

"Nova, I'm not interested in Chelsea or Lauren," he said sincerely. "They're ridiculous. I'm only interested in you."

At least now she knew their names. "I don't really care." She was surprised at how true that statement was. She didn't plan on getting to know this Ethan. She wouldn't be here long enough.

"Ouch." He seemed genuinely wounded. "I didn't mean to embarrass you. I'm really sorry."

"No, I just mean… it doesn't matter." Nova stammered, deciding that from this point on, she should just try not to talk.

After that, she smiled and said little. Ethan kept giving her questioning looks but remained glued to her side and ignored Chelsea and Lauren when they tried to start up another conversation.

When they sat down for dinner, he pulled out her chair and whispered in her ear, "You look beautiful, by the way."

Nova decided to cut him some slack. He was probably as nervous around her as she was around him, even if it was for different reasons. In retrospect, the looks on the ditzy twins' faces *had* been kind of funny. And they didn't seem like the sharpest tacks in the drawer, so they'd probably find some other poor guy to gush over by the end of the night.

Dinner seemed to drag on forever as the servers kept mixing up everyone's orders. Nova didn't care that she ended up with spaghetti and meatballs instead of the chicken parmesan she'd asked for. All she cared about was getting the party over with so she could retreat to the peace and quiet of her bedroom where she could think. Every minute in this timeline was dragging her farther and farther away from her old life and her connection to Marshall.

Nova was grateful when Celeste finally brought out the cake and everyone sang Happy Birthday. Maybe the night was finally coming to an end.

"Let me have everyone's attention!" Her mother was beaming. "Dayton and I have a surprise for Alana and Nova."

Nova looked at her dad, and he shrugged. Obviously it was going to be a surprise for him too. *Whatever it is, Mom, I don't want it. You can't keep me here.*

Celeste tapped her fork on a glass to quiet the last few talkers in the group. "Girls, I know you were probably hoping for cars, but your dad and I thought about it and decided to give you a lifelong memory instead." She caught Dayton's eye. "Day, would you like to tell them?"

He had just taken a swig of his iced tea and inhaled instead of swallowing, coughing half of it up. David was close by and pounded him on the back. When Dayton had recovered enough to speak, he waved at Celeste.

"You tell them, babe," he croaked.

"All right," she laughed. "Since your dad's recuperating from his near-death experience, I'll give you the news."

She motioned for her daughters to come forward. Nova wished there was a hole to fall into.

Celeste waited until the girls were sufficiently separated from the crowd and continued. "Before long, you'll both graduate and move on with your separate lives. You have these last couple of years together before that happens. So with that in mind, we've decided to give you a trip. Three weeks, anywhere in the world. Within reason, of course! No camping in the desert or hiking in the Himalayas! Dad and I will go along, but you're in charge of the itinerary—where we go and how long we stay there, it's all your choice. We want you to have this trip to look back on. Something amazing that you did together. The only catch is that you have to agree on where you want to go and make all the plans together."

An ecstatic Alana could barely contain herself, and everyone around her started talking at once, throwing out ideas all over the globe.

Alana ignored all of them, immediately declaring her choice. "Paris! I've always wanted to go, and as far as I'm concerned, we can stay there the whole three weeks!"

"Remember, it's not only up to you." Celeste laughed, turning her attention to Nova. "Well, honey?"

Nova stood there with her mouth hanging open until Ethan closed it for her, making the room explode with laughter. She felt her face go bright red. How could she think about a trip right now? She planned to get out of this reality as soon as she possibly could. As a matter of fact, if she walked out right now, what difference would it make? Nova glanced at the door, tempted to make a run for it. So her family and everyone at school would think she was crazy. No... what was the word Delilah loved to use? *Mental.* They'd think she'd gone mental. Nova had to suppress the urge to laugh out loud. That would be the final nail in her social coffin. Her eyes swept the room. Everyone was waiting for her answer.

"I'm, uh… could we… wait?" she stammered.

"WAIT?" Alana was incredulous. "Wait for what?"

"I just want to think about it." Nova looked down at her hands. Obviously her reaction wasn't what her mother had hoped for, but there was nothing she could do about that.

"Let's talk about this at home," her dad finally spoke up. "It's a big decision."

Alana frowned at her. "Way to bring down the party, little sister."

"Sorry." Nova responded quietly. "I just don't know where I want to go."

"Well, *I* want to go to Paris if you think you can manage. Rome would be okay too. Maybe we can hop around—Paris, Rome, London? Jump in any time." Alana pursed her lips and waited for an answer, tapping her foot impatiently.

"Please can we talk about this at home?" Nova pleaded. "I can't do it right now with everyone staring." Alana shook her head and turned away, ignoring her.

Ethan leaned in and whispered in Nova's ear, "Do you want to leave?"

"Yes," she responded, fighting tears. She hadn't had her sister back a whole day and they'd already had their first fight. Nova looked at Alana. *I wish I could go to Paris with you.*

Nova explained that she wasn't feeling well, and Celeste reluctantly agreed to let Ethan drive her home.

He took her hand, leading her out to the parking lot. "Well, that was awkward. No Paris, huh?"

"I don't know. I couldn't think with everyone watching me." Nova was trying not to cry outside of Mario's, but she felt as though the dam was about to burst.

Still holding her hand, he led her around to the passenger side of his pickup and opened the door for her. "Where to, hot girl?"

When he used his pet name for her for the first time in this reality, Nova stared at him through tears. Standing there holding her door, his hair falling slightly over one eye and his smile exposing the dimple in his cheek, he looked exactly like her Ethan. Nova threw her arms around his neck and kissed him tenderly. When she pulled away, he fell into a fit of coughing.

"Ethan—what?"

"Swallowed my gum—" he managed to choke out.

"Sorry."

Ethan recovered a little and grinned. "That's okay. I can always get more gum."

"No, I mean… I don't want you to think I'm, uh—"

"Amazing?" Ethan was still grinning. It was unnerving.

"Love starved or… I don't know." Nova wished she could stop blushing. "I mean, I don't usually do that."

"Really?" He pretended to think about that for a moment. "Bummer."

Nova jabbed him in the arm with her elbow and slid into the passenger seat.

Ethan ran around to the other side and hopped in. "Like I said, where to?"

His dark blue eyes met hers, and she wanted to kiss him again. So much for the whole "not getting to know him" thing. Right now, all she wanted to do was throw herself at him and tell him everything. He'd believed her before, so why wouldn't he again? *Stop it. As far as he's concerned, he's only known you a few hours!*

Nova looked away. "Just start this thing and let's get out of here before I have more to explain."

"Whatever you say, hot girl." She didn't have to look at him to know he was grinning from ear to ear. Ethan started the truck and pulled out of the parking lot. "So where do I point this manly truck?"

"Just take me home. It's been a weird night."

"I wouldn't call it weird. Well… yeah, I guess I

would. Okay, home it is. What are you doing tomorrow?"

"I don't know. Alana and Mom may drag me to the travel agency so they can shove bamboo shoots up my fingernails until I decide on a destination."

"Ouch! Well, what about after that? Can I call you?"

"Let me think about it," she answered quickly.

Ethan pulled onto Riverbank Road, four blocks from her house. Nova stared out the window, hoping to avoid any more conversation. As they rode along, she tried to sort out everything that had transpired in the last twenty-four hours.

Her dad's accident on the bridge had set into motion a chain of events that had brought her to this point. If he had never had the wreck, would she have ever found out about the Grant family gift? Nova couldn't decide if she was glad to know or if it would have been better to go through her life blissfully unaware of the power that lay dormant inside her. It had all started with the bridge. If the sanitation truck had crossed the line anywhere else, Dayton would probably have survived the crash, or maybe avoided the wreck completely. Their lives would have stayed on the same course and she most likely would never have known about Alana or the Grant family's ability to travel through time.

Nova marveled at the fact that she barely thought about the bridge anymore. Her dad's accident didn't even seem real now. It was more like a nightmare that lingered vaguely in her mind. Dayton Grant wasn't dead anymore, but Aunt Jean and Marshall were. Who would come back the next time she changed? And, more unsettling, who would she lose?

Nova continued to stare out the window, not really seeing the landscape, until they turned into her driveway.

"Are you thinking about it?" Ethan asked.

"What?" She couldn't remember what he'd asked her.

"Whether or not I can call you."

"Oh, sure." She already had her hand on the door handle and jumped out before the truck had come to a complete stop. She ran up the walkway and into the house without looking back to see if he was following. Once inside, Nova leaned against the front door and listened to the sound of the truck backing out of the driveway as she replayed the parking lot kiss in her mind. *All he has to do is call me "hot girl" and I'm all over him. I'm such an idiot.* If she was still here tomorrow, she'd probably have some explaining to do. *If* he even wanted to see her again after her bizarre behavior.

CHAPTER 5

Nova lay on her bed, staring at the ceiling. Pushing Ethan away would be hard. Maybe she shouldn't even try. She could confide in him again, just like last time. He hadn't been that hard to convince. It wasn't like she'd be messing him up for life or anything. He wouldn't even miss her when she switched timelines again. Maybe he'd still end up with the Nova from his timeline. The thought of him with another version of herself bothered her for some reason.

She closed her eyes, willing herself to relax, but it was no use. As far as the trip with Alana was concerned, Nova would have to stall somehow while she figured things out. Of course, she could just tell Alana that she belonged to a family of time travelers. How bad would that be? Maybe she'd be pretty cool about it.

Nova heard a car pull into the driveway.

Moments later, Alana came bursting in. "What was that all about? Why didn't you want to go to Paris? Or Rome? Or Venice? Or anywhere cool like that? Mom was practically in tears after you left. You didn't even seem excited. What's your problem?"

Nova jumped up, any thoughts of telling her sister out the window. "I didn't say I don't want to go. I just said I want to wait."

"That's the same thing! If you wanted to go, you would've said so. Or at least been a tiny bit happy that our parents want to take us on this epic trip anywhere in the world. We can go somewhere else if that's what this is all about. We don't have to stay in Paris the whole time. Where do *you* want to go?"

"I don't know. Maybe Willow…"

"North Carolina??" If Nova had suddenly grown a third eye, her sister's expression probably would have looked exactly as it looked now. She stared at Nova, speechless, her mouth hanging open.

Nova thought of Aunt Jean's comment about catching flies and laughed out loud, immediately clamping her hand over her mouth. *What's wrong with me?*

"This is funny to you?" Alana fumed.

"No, it's not funny." Before she could have another inappropriate reaction, Nova threw her arms around her sister. "I'd love to take a trip with you! Just give me a few days to decide, okay?"

Her sudden display of affection softened her sister's mood. Alana's eyes narrowed and she seemed to be deciding whether to still be mad or to accept that Nova wasn't going to ruin their trip.

Finally, she responded in a much calmer tone, "Okay. I'll tell Mom and Dad we're deciding. That's what we're doing, right?"

"Right." Nova stepped back, smiling. "I promise."

"Okay!" Her sister beamed. "But I'm learning French. Just so you know."

"I was kind of thinking about the Netherlands, so maybe you should learn Dutch."

"Very funny. Paris, London, Venice, and Rome. Those are your choices." She flopped down on Nova's bed. "Is everything okay? Really?"

"Everything's fine," Nova lied. "I'm just tired."

"This seems like more than *just tired*. Are you sure nothing's wrong? You're not still messed up over Steven, are you?"

Nova shook her head, making a mental note to find out who this guy was. She couldn't think of anyone at school named Steven. Maybe he wasn't in her grade.

"Because you'd tell me if you were, right, little sister?"

Alana was genuinely concerned. It was endearing. Nova had fantasized about moments just like this since finding Alana's file in her dad's office.

"Of course I'd tell you, Allie." As soon as the words were out, Nova felt a chill run up her spine. She'd called her sister Allie as if it were the most natural thing in the world. The truth was it had *felt* natural. Nova waited for a reaction from Alana, but none came.

"So tell me how it went with Ethan." Alana grinned. "I saw you in the parking lot. Nice lip-lock, little sister."

"Oh my God. Did Mom and Dad see me too?" Nova was mortified.

"Well… they didn't actually *see* you, but everyone enjoyed the pictures. I really love the Polaroid camera Chelsea gave me for my birthday."

"Wha—no! Tell me you're kidding!"

"Maybe I am, and maybe I'm not. I'll tell you after you give me details!" Alana seemed very pleased with herself. "David has a whole new respect for you, by the way."

"Oh my God."

"Calm down, I'm kidding."

"Don't do that! I've had enough crap to deal with tonight."

"Okay, little sister, so spill it. What happened with you and Ethan?"

"He called me hot girl, so I kissed him. That's all."

"Hot girl? That's what he said?"

Nova smiled. "Yeah."

"Interesting." Alana thought for a moment. "Wait. I get it. Exploding star, right?"

"Right."

"What a dork." Alana shook her head. "A cute dork. But still a dork. That's the best he could come up with?"

"I liked it. I guess you had to be there."

"I'll take your word for it. You can tell me the rest tomorrow. Besides, after the parking lot make-out scene, I have a pretty good idea how things are going." Alana laughed and headed for the door. "I'm going to bed. See you in the morning, hot girl," she threw over her shoulder as she breezed out of the room.

Within moments, Nova heard Alana talking on the phone, most likely to David. Her room was too far away for Nova to make out anything, so she tiptoed to the door and listened.

"I don't know. She says she's thinking about it. She's been weird all day, but she won't tell me what's wrong. And what's with my dad? He acted like I'd just come back from Mongolia this morning, then didn't say two words the whole time we were at Mario's."

Nova felt guilty about eavesdropping and crept back to her room. So much for acting normal. Obviously Alana thought she wasn't herself, but Nova had no idea how to behave around her sister, having no frame of reference. Frustrated, she lay back on her bed again. Maybe she should just march into her sister's room and tell her the truth.

Well, sis, I haven't been around you since three timelines ago because you were dead. Dad was excited to see you this morning, also because of the dead thing. Oh, and you have a little brother who looks a lot like you. He's nine years old. You can't meet him right now because I kind of erased him. But don't worry, we'll straighten it all out the next time we switch lives.

Nova grabbed a pair of sweatpants and a T-shirt and carried them into the bathroom. She filled the tub and lowered herself up to her shoulders. The warm water immediately began to pull the tension from her body. She took several slow, deep breaths, wishing she could just fall asleep right there and forget about everything. Even as her body relaxed, her mind refused to cooperate, shifting from her sister and Marshall to Ethan. The Ethan in this timeline was unsettling for some reason. Maybe she was the one making it different. She'd been standoffish in the last timeline, unlike this one, where she'd thrown herself at him in the parking lot. Maybe Ethan was exactly the same as before. He was just reacting to this *different* Nova.

She felt her cheeks flush as she thought about her mad dash to the house. Enduring the awkward moment when it came time to say good night would have been better. She wished she'd just gotten through it instead of running up the driveway like an idiot. He probably thought she was nuts.

Secretly, she hoped he'd show up at her window like he used to in her old life, but in this reality, Ethan didn't even know which one was hers. Thinking about the kiss at the window that night before she left for Willow reminded Nova of the promise she'd made to get to know him again if they weren't together in another timeline. Keeping that promise was proving to be complicated. It would be better to wait until she had straightened things out, then they could start over. Why start something when she didn't plan to stick around? But she wasn't sure she'd be able to follow through with keeping her distance, because she loved him, no matter which timeline she was in.

The water had slowly cooled to the uncomfortable point, so Nova dried off, put on the clothes she'd hung on the hook by the tub, tiptoed back to her room, and crawled into bed. Celeste always kept the house cool at night, so Nova snuggled down into the covers and closed her eyes. *I'll deal with all of this tomorrow,* she thought as she drifted off.

***

When Nova woke early the next morning, she thought for a moment that she was back in her former timeline—the one that was perfect, except for Alana. The illusion only lasted a second.

She sat up and rubbed her eyes. The alarm clock on her side table read 6:43 a.m. Her mom was usually in the kitchen by now, having coffee before her morning run. Nova sat perfectly still and listened, but the house seemed quiet. She jumped out of bed, cracked open her bedroom door, and looked into the dim hallway. A light was coming from underneath the office door. She tiptoed over and turned the knob. Dayton was sitting at the desk, engrossed in a book.

"Hi, Dad," she said quietly so not to wake anyone else.

"Good morning, firefly," he answered softly. "You're up early."

"What are you reading?"

"Come look."

Nova walked around the desk. It wasn't a book at all, but a journal of some kind. "Did you write that?"

"No. It was in my mother's things from the attic. I think she wrote this when she was young, before she met my father. There were several of them in her things. She talks a lot about losing someone, so that must be Daniel and the baby. I still can't figure out why Mother didn't tell me about them. And why did Aunt Jean tell you but not me?"

"I don't know. We were just talking in the kitchen and it came up, I guess. Maybe she figured I'd tell you. But then, all I could think about was traveling."

"I never understood before why my mother didn't try to save my father. Maybe she thought the same thing would happen and she'd lose me too."

"I think that's probably exactly what she thought."

Dayton closed the journal and looked at Nova. "I'm sorry my mother went through so much, but I don't understand why she never tried to fix any of it."

Nova started to point out that her dad hadn't gone back and tried again to save his other daughter, but she bit her tongue.

Dayton studied her for a moment. Apparently the irony dawned on him because he looked down at the journal and shook his head. "I know what you're thinking, firefly. I gave up too. I guess quitting runs in the family."

"You're not a quitter."

"All evidence to the contrary."

"Okay, fine. But it doesn't matter now. We're not going to quit this time. I know Marshall is meant to be with us. There's no doubt in my mind. That's why we have to make Grandma Kate helps us, even if she's afraid. She knows more about traveling than we do. She grew up hearing about it and probably experiencing it too, whenever someone in her family switched timelines. She has to know something we don't know. And… I think we need to tell Alana the truth. All of it."

"I agree that we need to go see Grandma Kate and ask for her help, but I don't want to tell your sister yet. It'll be hard enough seeing Mother and talking to her about Marshall. I can't deal with breaking this kind of news to Alana too. If all hell breaks loose around here, we're not going to be able to focus on what we need to do. Let's wait at least until we talk to your grandmother. Agreed?"

"I guess so. But we're going to have to tell Alana sooner or later."

"Not necessarily. If one of us travels, we may not need to tell her at all."

Her dad was right. Telling Alana could cause an emotional explosion that would make an already terrible situation even worse.

He said, "There's one more thing. No matter what happens, I don't think we should ever tell her about Marshall. I think she'd be devastated if she knew about him."

Nova thought for a moment, imagining how she'd feel in Alana's place if she found out that she was the reason her little brother had lost his chance at life. In reality, Nova *was* the reason Marshall was gone. And that knowledge was a knife through her heart. "Okay, we'll wait. And we won't tell her about Marshall."

"That's my girl." Dayton forced a smile. "I'll call Mother right now, before anyone else is up. Why don't you go back to bed for a while?"

He obviously wanted some privacy, so Nova gave him a quick hug and headed back to her room, quietly closing the door.

About fifteen minutes later, he stuck his head in. "It's all set. We'll leave in the morning."

"Where does Grandma Kate live?"

"Frederick, New Hampshire. It's the house we moved to when I was young. You went there when you were little, but I guess I had a falling out with Mother and we haven't been there since then." He shook his head. "So many years lost. It seems ridiculous to me that I didn't go see my own mother and let her get to know her grandkids. Now she may never know Marshall."

"Don't say that. We're gonna get him back."

"You're right, honey. Sorry."

"Okay. What about Mom and Alana? What if they want to come with us?"

"We won't tell them where we're going. I'll say we're going on a short research trip around the New England area, looking for settings for my next book. Celeste never wants to go on those. She thinks they're boring. Well, if past experience means anything. She never wanted to before. We'll just play it by ear with Alana. If she asks to go, we'll have to come up with something to change her mind."

"Okay." Nova tried to imagine manipulating her strong-willed sister but couldn't picture it.

"How about some breakfast with your old man?" He smiled in earnest.

"Sure."

For the rest of the morning, Nova could think of nothing but seeing her grandmother. She'd died when Nova was young before, and her memories of her had faded over the years. What she did recall was that Grandma Kate had seemed a little cold, almost stern. It was hard to believe that she and Aunt Jean were sisters. And yet, Aunt Jean had described Kate as fun-loving, so much like Dayton. Maybe she'd been that way when she was young, before Daniel and the baby. Nova had seen firsthand how quickly someone could slip into depression because that was exactly what had happened to her dad.

Around noon, Nova was itching for something to do to give her mind a rest from thinking so much about Marshall and Grandma Kate. She'd gone over and over everything she planned to say to her grandmother but still wasn't satisfied that it would be enough. If she didn't take a break, she felt as if her brain would explode. To make matters worse, Ethan had called twice that morning. She'd managed to be "busy" both times, but sooner or later she'd have to deal with him too.

Alana popped into Nova's room just before two. "Get ready! Mom's taking us shopping for luggage! You know, for our *trip*?"

"Not right now. I'm kinda busy," Nova lied.

"Yeah, I can see that." Alana made an elaborate show of looking around the room.

"I mean I'm getting ready to do something."

"What would that be, little sister? Paint your nails? Wash your hair? Split an atom?"

"I thought I'd go to the library and get some books about France and Italy," Nova lied again. She had no intention of going to the library, but since it was within walking distance and her mom and Alana were going shopping, who would know?

Alana perked up considerably. "Oh. That's great! I can go with you!"

Crap. Now what? Nova racked her brain. "Why don't you go with Mom to pick out luggage for both of us and I'll get the books and bring them back here? We can look at them tonight."

"Perfect!" Alana beamed. "I knew you'd get into it eventually. It'll be a great trip." She hugged Nova tightly.

Nova had the overwhelming urge to burst into tears. She held her breath and forced a smile. "Let's tell Mom about the library."

"Sure thing." Alana grabbed Nova's hand and took off up the hallway to the kitchen, where Celeste was waiting.

Eyeing Nova's sweatpants and T-shirt, Celeste asked, "Aren't you going with us?" She sounded disappointed.

"It's okay," Alana said cheerfully. "I'm picking out luggage for both of us and Nova's going to the library to get books on Europe so we can decide where we're going!"

"I like that!" Celeste smiled warmly. "I knew you'd come around, honey."

"Yeah. I guess I'm getting excited about it." Nova loved seeing her mom so happy.

"We'll be gone a while. Why don't you open your presents from the party?" Celeste suggested.

"Sure." She had no interest in gifts right now, but it was something to do to kill some time.

The packages were still stacked on the coffee table in the den. Plopping down on the floor, she picked up one to unwrap. It was from Chelsea—a Polaroid camera just like Alana's. Nova pictured the two girls flirting with Ethan and wondered which one was Chelsea. Pulling the camera out of the box, she loaded the film, flipped it around to face her, and snapped. The undeveloped photo shot out almost immediately and dropped to the floor. Nova leaned in close, watching her image gradually appear. All she could think of was how much Marshall would have loved it.

"Oh, you got a Polaroid too!" Her mom had walked into the den, looking for her car keys. "I used to have one of those, but they're hard to find now, I imagine. I wonder where she got them." Celeste leaned over and watched as the picture finished developing.

"It looks like a mug shot, doesn't it?" Nova observed.

"I wouldn't say that… exactly." Her mom laughed. "But smile next time."

"Are you looking for these?" Nova asked, fishing the keys from under the presents.

"Yes! Thank you. Are you sure you don't want to come along? I'd figured we'd have a girls' outing. We can have lunch, go to the mall for luggage, and then stop for ice cream afterward."

"I really want to go to the library. I'll be sure to get lots of information we can use for the trip. Just pick me out something nice."

"Okay, honey. We'll be back in a few hours."

When the front door slammed a minute or two later, Nova assumed that they had left until Alana stuck her head in the den.

"Your hot guy is here," she whispered, grinning.

CHAPTER 6

"Ethan's here?" Nova jumped up. "I can't see him right now!" What was he doing just showing up like this?

"You want me to tell him to leave?" Alana asked softly.

"Yes—wait—no!" Nova looked down at the sweatpants with the rip in the knee that she'd slept in.

"Jeez, make up your mind!" Alana stood there tapping her fingers on the doorframe. "Nova!" she mouthed almost silently. "He's in the kitchen with Mom, so decide. Tick, tock!"

"Oh my God. Tell him to wait."

Nova dashed down the hall to her room and kicked off the sweatpants. She yanked open the dresser drawers and found a pair of shorts and a lavender top to change into. Catching a glimpse of herself in the mirror, she gasped out loud. "My hair!"

She grabbed a hairband and pulled it into a loose ponytail, letting some pieces dangle around her face. It would have to do. Nova took a moment to collect herself, waiting for her pulse to slow down. She had to stop reacting this way to Ethan, but every time she was around him, she felt herself bonding with this timeline more and more. Giving up and staying would be so easy, but then Marshall would be gone forever. Nova couldn't let her resolve crumble. Ethan would understand if she could tell him the truth. In the meantime, she'd go through the motions and try to stick with the plan.

Nova took a deep breath and walked up the hall and into the kitchen.

Ethan was sitting at the table, listening to Alana and Celeste chatter on about the trip. He stood, obviously relieved, when he saw Nova.

"Ethan, what are you doing here?" Nova asked a little too bluntly.

He grinned. "I thought we could go to Burger Barn and hang out."

"Well, uh…" Nova blushed, thinking about the last time they were there.

"Go ahead, Nova. Ethan can drive you to the library too, so you don't have to walk back carrying a bunch of books," Alana suggested cheerfully.

Nova gave her smug sister a withering look but saw no way to get out of it now. The truth was that she loved every minute she was with Ethan, even if he was a little different this time around. He'd captured her heart in her former timeline and still had it.

"I guess I could go for a while," she agreed.

"Good! My truck's outside." He pushed open the screen door and stood aside, waiting for her to go first.

"In the backyard?" she asked, amused.

"Nope. On the street by the bus stop."

He took her hand as they walked across the yard. She stumbled a little and his grip tightened, making her heart beat faster. Would he always have this effect on her, she wondered? Nova realized that she was grinning like an idiot. Alana was right—she was making it too easy, but there was nothing she could do about it. The second she got around him, she lost all of her resolve to keep her distance. All she wanted to do was to throw her arms around him and kiss him right there with her mom and Alana watching from the kitchen window, their mouths hanging open. The thought made her laugh out loud, followed by the familiar sensation of her cheeks going bright red.

"What's funny?" he asked.

Not trusting an intelligent response to come out of her mouth, Nova shrugged, still smiling. Ethan's truck was parked a short distance from the bus stop, just out of sight of the house.

He opened the passenger door. "Hop in, hot girl!"

"That's not gonna work every time, you know," Nova pointed out as she climbed onto the seat, still feeling flustered.

"No idea what you're talking about." He grinned, shut the door, and jogged around to his side of the truck. As he slid in beside her, he leaned over and kissed her gently. "My turn." He smiled.

"My mom's probably watching us!"

"She can't see us from here. That's why I parked in this exact spot. All part of my diabolical plan."

Nova's heart felt as if it would beat out of her chest. She wanted to say something witty, but her brain wasn't cooperating. This timeline kept getting more and more complicated. The sooner she straightened things out, the better it would be for everyone.

"Let's just go, okay? I'm hungry." The truth was that her stomach was in knots and she'd be lucky to choke anything down.

"Yes ma'am!" He laughed, starting the truck.

The last time they'd been to the Burger Barn, Amanda had come in with Brian and… David!

"That's why he looked so familiar!" Nova blurted out.

"Who?" Ethan asked.

"David! I knew I'd seen him before!" Nova continued, oblivious to the fact that she was making no sense.

"Who are you talking about? Alana's boyfriend?"

"Yeah… sorry." *Why can't I control what pops out of my mouth?* She smiled sheepishly at Ethan. "Just ignore me. I can't explain."

"Whatever you say, hot girl." He laughed. "Should I be jealous?"

"No! I just saw him somewhere. Before they dated." *Stop talking, you idiot!* Nova giggled nervously.

"Okay. Because I'm already a little jealous about Steven, just so you know." He nudged her arm playfully.

"You don't need to worry about him. Trust me." It was the truth. She wouldn't be able to pick Steven out of a lineup if her life depended on it. "What about you? Any girls in your past I should worry about?"

"Wow. Where do I begin? So many."

Nova punched him in the shoulder. "Never mind."

"Don't worry. There's nobody worth mentioning."

"What about Delilah?"

"Is that the girl who hangs out with Joanna Romano?"

"Probably," Nova answered.

"I don't know her, but Joanna's in my biology lab. And no, I haven't dated her either. How about you? Besides Steven, are there any old boyfriends I should know about?"

Nova pretended to think about that. "Well… there was this one guy. Mason. But I dumped him."

"Why?" Ethan was clearly interested.

"He wouldn't share his peanut butter and jelly sandwich with me and hogged the play stove when we had kitchen time."

"I'm guessing preschool?" He grinned.

"Kindergarten."

"Where is this Mason guy? I might have to talk to him about the whole not sharing thing."

"Good luck. I think his family moved to Montana or South Dakota. Somewhere like that."

"I guess I'll let him off the hook then." Ethan put his hand on her arm as he drove.

He knows what he does to me! Nova thought, determined not to react.

They pulled up to the Burger Barn, and parked in almost the exact space they'd been in the last time they were there. He'd been upset that she was going to Aunt Jean's, worried that she'd do something that would change everything. He'd been right. For the most part, that was exactly what had happened.

Ethan jumped out of the truck and ran around to her side to open her door. As she climbed out, he kissed her cheek.

"Ethan…" Nova wanted to tell him not to bother, that she wasn't going to be here that long. How many times would she have to go through this with him—keeping him at a distance and pretending not to know him while wishing she could let her guard down? She felt weary from the emotional strain.

"Don't worry. I don't expect a lot. I'm just happy to be with you."

"It's okay. I just need to go slow."

Was this all their relationship would ever be—starting over time after time? Nova suddenly felt as if the dam was about to burst, and since she didn't want to stand in the Burger Barn parking lot sobbing, she took off ahead of him. Her emotions seemed to constantly leap from one extreme to the other. Her apparent lack of control was alarming to say the least.

"Wait up!" he called, jogging after her.

"Sorry to be so weird today."

"That's okay. I like a mysterious woman." He smiled again, exposing that maddeningly adorable dimple.

"Oh my God." Nova shook her head, blushing again.

They grabbed a booth at the back and ordered chili cheese fries just like before. Nova almost commented on it but caught herself just in time.

"What are you thinking about?" Ethan asked. "You looked like you started to say something."

"I was just having a déjà vu moment."

"Oh. I thought maybe you were gonna say you were having a great time, or you're crazy about me. Something like that." He reached across the table and pushed a strand of hair from her face. "You're beautiful."

"Thanks," was all she could get out. This Ethan was unnerving. It was hard to keep her head on straight around him. She suddenly realized that being with him was probably the only thing holding her together. "Ethan, I *do* like you. Don't give up on me, okay?"

"No way," Ethan responded sincerely. "I really like you too."

For the next half an hour, they talked about school. Nova found out that his locker was in a different hall than hers, but he had walked down her hall after lunch every day for the whole school year just to see her. He'd been late to Mrs. Fincher's biology lab so many times she'd threatened to fail him. In spite of that, he had an A-minus in the class. *She probably has a crush on you too,* Nova thought, smiling.

After they finished the fries, Nova suggested they free up the table for someone else, since at least a dozen people were standing at the front, waiting to sit down. When they were back in the truck, she sat as close to the door as possible, determined to avoid another intimate moment. She couldn't afford to get distracted from her goal—changing timelines and getting Marshall back.

"Where to now, hot girl?"

"The library, I guess." Nova moaned. She dreaded going through the motions of planning a trip she was never going to take with her sister.

"You're still not excited about it?" he asked.

"Not really," she answered honestly. "But Alana's excited enough for both of us."

"Why don't you want to go? If my parents offered me a trip to Europe, I'd be all over it."

"I just... I'm busy, that's all."

"Busy?" He laughed. "Doing what? I mean, besides falling in love with me and eating all my fries."

Nova gulped down the last of her drink and giggled, immediately turning red for what felt like the hundredth time.

"Don't do that!" she managed to choke out. He took her empty cup and tossed it out the window into a garbage can that was about three feet away on the sidewalk. "Sorry. You're just so much fun to mess with." He grinned.

"Yeah, it's a gift," she quipped.

"Seriously though. What are you so busy doing?"

"What are you, six? Why are you asking so many questions?"

"Just trying to figure you out, hot girl," he answered, clearly amused.

"Okay, fine. I'm working on something with my dad."

Ethan turned and faced her. "Oh yeah? What?"

"I c-can't really talk about it. Sorry. I'd love to tell you, but when my dad's working on a *project,* I can't say what it is. You understand, don't you?"

"Sure." He put his hand on her arm, smiling as he started the truck. "Library it is then. Maybe when you start planning, you'll get happy about the trip. Or you could take me with you. That'd work too."

She laughed. "No chance. Mom and Dad would never go for that."

"Okay then." He stuck out his lower lip in a pretend pout. "Let's hit the library. Can't think of any place I'd rather hang out on a beautiful summer day."

"Shut up." She giggled.

CHAPTER 7

They practically had the library to themselves, so the young librarian was eager to help them find the information they were looking for. There were literally hundreds of travel books available, and he seemed determined to bring them every one. Nova and Ethan chose a table near the windows and leafed through a dozen or so books. Every time they found one that seemed perfect, the librarian would drop another two or three in front of them. Finally, Nova insisted that they had all they needed and the disappointed young man trudged back to the main desk to wait for his next victim.

Nova moaned. "This is too much. I'll never read all this. I'm just gonna tell Alana we'll go wherever she wants and leave the planning to her. It doesn't matter anyway." Nova realized too late that she had put her foot in her mouth again.

"What's up with you? You act like you're not even going," Ethan whispered.

"Just ignore me. It's been a weird couple of days." She knew that was a lame explanation. "Something going on with my sister and me."

She was apparently talking too loudly because the librarian cleared his throat to get her attention and put his finger to his lips. Nova looked around to see if anyone else had come in, but there was no one in the building.

"Sorry." She flashed the young man a sweet smile, which seemed to please him immensely. She leaned over the table and whispered, "Maybe we should get out of here."

"Sounds good to me," Ethan agreed.

Nova checked out several European travel books and a map of Paris, which she knew her sister would particularly like.

"Do you want to give me your number, you know, in case something else comes in?" the librarian asked hopefully.

"That's okay. I'm sure this is enough," Nova responded quickly.

As soon as they were back in the truck, Ethan shook his head and backed out without speaking.

"What?" Nova asked.

"I was just thinking that guy in there had a crush on you." He chuckled.

"You think? He was kind of cute in an 'I read books all day and never get out in the sun' kind of way. I may have to keep him as a backup."

"Sure. He's definitely your type."

Nova punched him lightly in the arm as they pulled up to a stop sign. There were no other cars around, and Ethan kissed her suddenly, catching her off guard. Obviously sitting next to the door wasn't helping. Before she could say something, another car pulled up behind them and Ethan drove through the intersection, turning onto her street two blocks down.

"What are you doing tomorrow?" Ethan asked.

"I'm going out of town with my dad for a few days."

"You're leaving tomorrow?" he asked when he pulled into her driveway a couple of minutes later.

"Yeah." She decided not to mention the kiss. "We're leaving early, like six o'clock."

"So I won't see you for what… three days?" He frowned.

"I'm not sure. Probably at least that long." Nova looked down at the books in her lap. When she looked up again, he was studying her.

"Anything you want to tell me?"

"No. I'll be back in a few days, okay? I promise," she lied. Maybe she would be back, but she hoped not.

"Okay. I'll see you then."

He kissed her again, lingering longer than he had before. Nova put her arms around his neck and kissed him back. If this was the last time she was going to see him in this timeline, she wanted a real kiss, like the ones she'd had in the old life. After all, this was still Ethan, her Ethan. Even if he didn't know that.

When Nova pulled away, she nearly jumped out of her skin. Alana had her face pressed up against the passenger's window.

"Nice lip action, you two!" She grinned, obviously pleased with herself.

Nova rolled down her window. "Alana! Don't do that!" she blurted out, feeling her face go bright red.

"Lighten up, little sister." Alana laughed, turning her attention to Ethan. "You know, my dad has a shotgun in the house."

Nova looked at Ethan, mortified. His face appeared redder than hers felt.

"Hi, Alana," he managed awkwardly.

Nova opened her door quickly, nearly knocking her sister down. "I'll call you later, Ethan."

She quickly gathered up the books, grabbed Alana by the arm, and ushered her into the house. Nova dropped the books on the floor in the den and turned on her sister. "Why did you do that? It was embarrassing!"

"Like I said before, lighten up," Alana answered, still obviously amused. "I wanted to show you the luggage Mom and I bought."

"Fine. Whatever. Just don't *ever* do that again. Okay?"

"If you don't want people gawking at you, don't make out in our driveway. Jeez." Alana giggled. She picked up one of the travel books and started leafing through it.

"We weren't making out. We were just kissing,"

Nova replied, still annoyed.

"We must have different definitions of making out because what you and Ethan were doing was it," Alana pointed out smugly. "I take full credit, you know. I'm the one who set you up."

Nova rolled her eyes. "Good grief. Just show me the freaking luggage."

Alana dropped the book on the floor with the others and took off down the hall with Nova on her heels. The new luggage was arranged carefully in Nova's room as if it were still in the department store. There were two carry-on-sized rolling suitcases, two larger ones, also on wheels, and a couple of satchels. One set was a light-blue tweed and the other was a deep plum color.

"You bought a lot," Nova commented.

Alana beamed. "Mom and I decided that three weeks isn't enough time, so we're going for a whole month! Apparently we have some relatives in England on her side—cousins or something like that. They used to live near here but moved about ten years ago. And get this, they're renovating an old castle! Mom said you and I can fly into London and they'll pick us up. We'll stay with them for a week or two and they'll take us around, showing us the sights. Then Mom and Dad will come and we'll take the train from London to Paris! We can stay in Paris a few days, then rent a car and go wherever the spirit moves us!"

All Nova managed to get out was, "That's… unbelievable." It sounded like an amazing trip. She was sorry they wouldn't actually be going.

Celeste stuck her head in the door and beamed at Nova, clearly just as excited as Alana. "I see she told you!"

"It sounds incredible," Nova replied, feeling as if she was going to burst into tears any second.

Celeste took her emotional reaction as excitement and ran over to hug her. "It'll be a trip you girls will always remember. Richard and Maureen are going to let you help pick out some furnishings for their guest rooms. They're planning to turn the castle into a bed-and-breakfast. I guess you'll be their first visitors!"

"It really does sound wonderful," Nova said sincerely.

"So which set do you want?" Alana asked.

"Set?"

"The luggage. Which color do you want?" Alana asked impatiently. "I thought I'd go ahead and throw some things in mine."

Nova tried to act as enthusiastic as her sister, but Alana set the bar pretty high. She looked as though she were about to combust any second.

"I don't really care. You pick," Nova answered.

"I'll take the plum then. I know you like blue," Alana replied happily.

Nova impulsively hugged her sister. "It all sounds perfect. I can't think of anything I'd love to do more."

Alana seemed immensely pleased at Nova's apparently changed attitude. Celeste had moved their travel schedule up and already bought their plane tickets for nine days away. If Nova was going to switch timelines, she'd have to do it before then or she'd be stuck going to Europe, and there was no telling what would happen then. All through dinner that evening, one thought played over and over in her mind—*If I get Marshall back, and everyone else is here, I'll never travel again.*

CHAPTER 8

Dayton didn't waste any time bringing up their "research" trip at dinner. Based on his demeanor, he had already talked to Celeste about their new travel dates and was feeling the same sense of urgency as Nova.

"I thought I'd get on the road to do some research. Just for a few days. I'll be back long before the girls leave for London. Anyone interested in coming with me? I know your mom isn't." He winked at Celeste, obviously trying his best to act *normal.*

"Day, I love you, but you know how I feel about those trips." Celeste chuckled.

"Yes, I do." He smiled, relieved.

"I'll go, Dad." Nova tried to sound nonchalant.

"A road trip?" Alana perked up. "New York, maybe? I could use some new clothes for Europe!"

"No. I thought I'd drive up to Vermont, possibly New Hampshire. I'm figuring out the setting for my next book. I want to do some research on the history of a few areas. You know, go through historical records. Check out the libraries. That kind of thing."

Alana wrinkled her nose. "Wow. Kill me. No thanks. Oops… did I just say that out loud?"

"Ouch. Nova, looks like it's just you and me!" Dayton smiled, relief written all over his face.

Alana's remark lightened Dayton's mood considerably, and he was still chuckling about it when the table was cleared. Nova loved it—all of them together and everyone happy. If Marshall had been there, it would have been the perfect life. *This is what I want. I don't care about being rich. I just want my family, my* whole *family... and Ethan.*

Dayton whispered to Nova, "That worked out well, didn't it?"

Nova nodded and glanced at her sister, who was taking the dishes off of the table.

Her mom was loading the dishwasher, but paused and looked at Dayton. "You should go see your mother while you're up that way. You haven't seen her in years, Day. She won't be here forever, and you won't always have the chance to talk about whatever it is you two were fighting about."

Dayton's face lost its jovial expression. He cleared his throat and mumbled something about talking to Grandma Kate before taking off down the hall to his office.

Celeste put her hand on Nova's arm. "Make him go see his mother. It's ridiculous to let a disagreement keep you from your family. She hasn't seen you since you were about five years old. I know she'd love to."

"We'll go see her, Mom. I promise." Nova headed down the hall and stopped at the office door. It was locked. "Dad? Can I come in?"

She heard the lock click and opened the door. Her dad motioned for her to come inside and closed the door behind her.

"I can't believe she brought up my mother. Do you think she knows something?" he asked anxiously.

Nova shook her head emphatically. "There's no way she could. And why haven't you talked to Grandma Kate in years?"

"How would I know? The fight we had before was about going back to save Alana. But your sister's alive in this timeline, so what could we be fighting about now?" He started pacing back and forth. "I guess it could be about the family. We argued about that too. I hated that she wouldn't have anything to do with the rest of the Grants. I guess I just didn't realize that I wouldn't get along with my mother no matter which timeline I was in."

"We'll find out what the problem was when we get there. You can say you're sorry about whatever it is. Let's stay focused, okay?"

"Okay, firefly. You're right. Besides, she seemed fine on the phone, like she was really glad I called. We'll work things out with her." Dayton looked relieved. "It was just a shock to hear we haven't spoken in so long. That's all. I'm okay now. I'm beginning to wonder though… will there be any timeline where everyone is alive and getting along?"

"What was it Aunt Jean said? There are an infinite number of possibilities," Nova pointed out.

"Yeah. Eventually we'll find the right one or die trying, right?"

"I hope so. The 'finding the right one' part. Not the 'die trying' part."

For some morbid reason, that struck them as terribly funny. Nova laughed so hard she finally had to sit down. Having a good laugh made her feel better, more optimistic.

"Go get your things together," he said, still laughing. "I want to leave early."

Nova hugged him and headed to her room to pack. She pulled her new satchel out of the closet and loaded it with enough clothes to last a week. If things went well with Grandma Kate, there was no telling how long they'd be there. Nova felt an excitement that she hadn't experienced since before realizing Marshall was gone. Grandma Kate had grown up with a family of travelers. She could explain what Evelyn had been talking about in her journal. There were "infinite possibilities," according to Aunt Jean. Nova just needed the one that would take her back to get her little brother.

The thought of seeing her grandmother after all these years was a little unsettling. Would Kate be the somber woman Nova remembered from her early childhood? Aunt

Jean had obviously loved her sister, still remembering her as a young girl. Nova made the decision to have an open mind. Besides, as long as Grandma Kate agreed to help them, it didn't matter what she was like.

Unable to shut off her brain, Nova lay in bed for hours, thinking about Marshall. *I'm coming to get you, kiddo,* she promised as she finally drifted off.

Nova heard Marshall calling her.

"Nova! Come on!"

She couldn't see him in the pitch dark. "Where are you?" There was no answer, so she tried again. "Marshall, where are you?"

This time he sounded farther away. "I'm here!"

Nova's eyes adjusted to the darkness, and she saw that she was in the hallway outside of her room at Willow Hill. She heard the clock ticking. It was funny that she'd never actually seen it even though she'd been all over most of the house.

She stood for a moment, listening, but there were no other sounds. The others must be sleeping. She started down the hallway toward the staircase, making a mental note to look for the clock later. The unsettling thought crossed her mind that the sound could be a figment of her imagination and not really there at all. Why did she only hear it at night? She shook off that thought. Of course it was there... somewhere.

Her feet were bare, and the wood floor felt wonderfully cool. Nova seemed to glide over it with little effort, like a car hydroplaning along a slick road.

"Marshall, where are you?"

She listened, still gliding along, but there was no response. She came to the stairs and descended them two at a time. Maybe he was at the barn. He loved the horses. It would be just like him to sneak out in the middle of the night with a bag of carrots. She could picture him going from stall to stall, each horse reaching out with a velvety muzzle to snatch a treat from his outstretched hands.

Nova ran through the empty kitchen and out the back door. The dew-laden grass tickled her feet as she glided effortlessly down the sloping yard toward the barn. She heard the horses snorting and stomping their feet, anxious to be fed. Maybe her little brother was in the loft, throwing hay down through the chutes like he had with Justin so many times.

Nova entered the barn and listened, but suddenly everything was quiet. She slowly made her way down one side of the dimly lit aisle, stopping at each stall and peering inside. One by one, each horse eyed her suspiciously, as if asking what she was doing there at that time of night.

"Where are you, Marshall?" she called. There was no answer. "Marshall, where are you!"

Halfway up the other side of the aisle, Nova noticed a plaque on the stall door next to the wash bay. It read "Bo." He was Marshall's favorite horse.

"Where's my little brother, Bo?"

He looked at her with gentle brown eyes and tossed his head. In the back corner of his stall was a dark shape in the bedding. Nova strained to see but couldn't make out what it was with so little light. She slowly unlatched the door and stepped inside. Bo snorted and backed away as she crept over to the crumpled figure. With a sense of dread, Nova touched rough canvas. It was a burlap bag, apparently left in the stall by accident. Relieved, Nova threw it into the aisle and stepped back out, latching the door behind her.

She stood quietly, listening for any sound that would lead her in the right direction. Something felt wrong. Why wouldn't he answer her? She looked back at the horse, standing at the back of his stall watching her.

"Where's Marshall?" she asked again.

Then she heard it—Marshall's voice calling to her from far away.

"Nova, where are you? I want to go home..."

CHAPTER 9

Nova jolted awake, her T-shirt damp with perspiration and her heart pounding. Her dad was standing in her doorway.

"Dad… oh my God. What are you doing? You scared me!"

"Better get up, firefly. It's five o'clock. Are you okay?"

She shoved the covers back and rubbed her eyes, trying to rid her mind of the dream. "I'm fine. Just had a weird dream. I'm up."

"You don't look like you feel well. We can put this off a day or two if you want."

"No, I'm not sick. I don't want to wait," Nova answered quickly.

"Okay," he said, frowning, obviously put off by her disheveled appearance. "Meet me in the kitchen when you're ready."

After showering and drying her hair, Nova felt a little more awake and anxious to get on the way. Dayton was waiting in the kitchen for her, two bowls of cereal already poured. They scarfed them down, loaded Celeste's Volvo, and pulled out of the driveway before anyone else was even awake. It occurred to Nova that she might never see this version of her mother again. The thought made her sad and she considered asking her dad to turn around so she could say goodbye, just in case. Of course, her mom would have no idea why she was making such a point of it. As far as she knew, Nova and Dayton were only going to be gone a few days. And she had the trip to plan, so she'd barely notice their absence.

I hope you're the same next time, Mom, Nova thought. She'd have to add that to her growing list labeled, "Things I'll Make Sure I Have in the Next Timeline." She smiled at the thought.

"I see you're feeling better," her dad said.

"Yes, I am. I was thinking about traveling. Do you think it'll happen at Grandma Kate's?"

"I seriously doubt it. I hope you're not in for a letdown. Your grandmother can be… challenging."

"I'm not worried. I know I can get through to her."

"Whatever you say, firefly," he replied, not sounding at all convinced.

"Seriously, Dad. I have great powers of persuasion." Nova giggled, not sure why she was suddenly in such a good mood. Maybe it was because they were finally doing something instead of just talking about it.

"No argument there." Dayton sighed. "Just don't get your hopes up too much. I have years of experience in more than one timeline to back up my opinion about my mother. She's not like her sister."

"I know." Anxious to change the subject, Nova asked, "How does Mom feel about driving the Mustang for a couple of days?"

He smiled. "She tried to act like she was dreading it, but secretly I think she's excited. Besides, if a miracle happens and we get what we need from your grandmother, we won't be gone that long."

Before long, they were driving through Hartford toward Boston. Nova closed her eyes and leaned her head against the headrest. It felt good to have a plan and she was eager to get to Grandma Kate's, but the stress of losing Marshall had exhausted her. For some reason, she thought about her trip to the attic with her little brother, feeling guilty that she'd used him to search for answers after her dad had returned from the dead. Marshall had been so excited to spend time with her.

Nova shook off the memory. No point dwelling on regrets because that would only make it more difficult to concentrate on the problem at hand. "When you're back, I'll make it up to you, kiddo," she whispered.

"Did you say something?" Dayton asked.

"Just thinking out loud." She closed her eyes again and tried to relax. As they continued driving, she allowed the motion of the Volvo and the sound of the road to lull her to sleep for the two-and-a-half-hour ride to their exit.

The next thing she knew, Dayton was nudging her arm. "Nova, wake up! We're here."

Still groggy from napping so long in the car, Nova rubbed her eyes and peered out the window. "This is Frederick?"

"Yep. This is where I grew up." Dayton smiled, taking the right fork onto High Street. "It looks exactly like I remember it. Of course, towns like this don't seem to change."

"It's beautiful."

Clapboard buildings and homes lined the road until they reached a roundabout with a bandstand in the center. Circling around, they continued down the main street through town, almost immediately passing an ice cream shop next to a wood-sided building with a large plaque that said "Willow."

"Dad, look at the name of that shop! It's a sign." She smiled broadly.

He laughed. "Sure, it is."

"No, really! Willow? What are the chances there would be a store with a sign out front that said 'Willow'?"

"Okay, I get it! I hope you're right."

They continued past old brick buildings, some with plaques designating them as historic and giving the dates they were constructed and what their original purposes were before modern times had relegated them to clothing stores and antique shops. One stately building towered above the others, although *towered* was probably stretching it, as the imposing edifice was only about four stories tall. But it wasn't the size that caught Nova's eye. It was the name, proudly displayed in bold letters. *ODD FELLOWS HALL.*

"Really? Odd fellows?" Nova laughed.

"Yeah. I know it sounds weird, but it was a big deal in our family many years ago. The organization was started in Manchester, England, but Thomas Wildley established an independent order in Baltimore in 1819. One of his associates who helped get it started was William Grant."

"Let me guess, one of my ancestors?"

"Right." Dayton laughed. "So I guess that explains a lot."

"Yeah. I always knew our family was odd. I just didn't know they made it official."

"Yeah, well, now you know," he said, still laughing.

"You seem to know a lot about it. Anything you want to confess?" Nova grinned.

"You mean am I an odd fellow?" He was clearly amused. "Well, yes and no. Yes, I can be pretty odd. Look at what I do for a living, not to mention being part of this strange family. But no, I'm not *officially* odd."

"Just checking. So what did it mean to be an 'odd fellow'?"

"I guess you'd call it a kind of fraternity that looks out for each other and embraces the philosophy of treating other people the way you'd want to be treated. That's a simplistic definition, but true. They were all about character and doing good works that benefited others."

"That's pretty cool. So why aren't you an odd fellow?"

"Who says I'm not?" He chuckled.

"You did."

"I said I wasn't *official.*"

"Okay. You're not an *official* odd fellow. But just so

you know, I've always thought of you as kind of odd."

Dayton threw his head back and laughed. "Thanks, honey. That means a lot."

They continued down High Street, passing out of the main part of town and into a residential area of old, well-maintained homes. Most of them were clapboard, many with white picket fences surrounding manicured lawns and gardens. When they turned onto Harvard Street, Nova noticed that most of the seemingly historic houses sat back farther from the road. Two older women strolling along the sidewalk watched them curiously as they drove by. Nova wondered if either of them knew her grandmother. For all she knew, one of them could *be* Grandma Kate. It had been so long since Nova had seen her, she may not even recognize her.

Dayton caught the expression on her face and patted her arm. "Don't worry. I think you'll know her when you see her."

Nova doubted that was true but nodded anyway. Harvard Street came to a dead end about three hundred feet ahead of them, and she wondered if her dad had made a wrong turn until he steered the car into a driveway on the right, barely visible from the road. Nova hadn't even noticed it because of the dense vegetation growing up around it. A thick layer of leaves concealed what might have been a gravel driveway years ago. The tires made a crunching sound as they rolled over rocks and fallen branches while low-hanging tree limbs scraped against the roof. They rounded a curve and passed a rickety mailbox that displayed the name *GRANT* in faded gold letters.

"Jeez, why doesn't she cut some of this back? I can't believe the mail carrier has to come in here," Nova remarked.

"I think he probably parks his truck and walks up. My mother likes her privacy. I doubt she gets much mail anyway." Her dad had taken on a somber tone.

"It's all right. She'll be glad to see you," Nova reassured him.

"Let's hope so, firefly."

The driveway straightened, and they broke free of the dense shrubbery, finally able to see the surprisingly large and immaculately maintained two-story clapboard home ahead of them. A deep porch spanned the entire width of the front of the house, which appeared to have been freshly painted a crisp white with a deep-red door. Blooming bushes bordered the front and sides. Nova recognized some of them as azaleas because she had helped her mom plant them in their yard. The hanging baskets of flowers along the porch reminded her of Ethan's house.

"Wow. After the overgrown driveway, I expected it to look run down or something. This is beautiful! Is everyone in our family rich? Except us, of course."

"Pretty much. But my mother didn't get all of this from traveling since she refused to have any part of it. My dad's parents were wealthy and left her a fortune when they died. As far as the rest of the Grants go, let's just say that traveling can be very profitable. Of course, I wouldn't know."

"That's okay. I like our house," Nova said sincerely.

"Me too, firefly," Dayton said, smiling. "Like I said, Mother likes her privacy. I think the driveway is meant to put people off."

"It works." Nova chuckled. When her dad didn't respond, she put her hand on his arm. "She really will be happy to see you. She's your mom."

Nova's point was proven about ten seconds later. Dayton turned off the motor and had just opened his door when Kate appeared on the porch, beaming. Nova found it hard to believe that this frail-looking woman was Aunt Jean's younger sister. Unlike her robust sister, Kate seemed delicate, even fragile. Her belted dress accentuated her slight frame, and her once-golden-blond hair, pulled into a neat bun, was streaked with gray. As they came closer, Nova recognized the same hazel eyes that Dayton, Alana, and Marshall shared, but Kate's had none of their life in them.

This was the sister Aunt Jean had described as fun-loving and pretty, full of the Grant sparkle? A lifetime of loss had obviously taken its toll.

Kate gripped the rail as she descended the stairs to meet them. "Day!" was all she managed to get out before starting to cry.

Clearly taken aback, Dayton strode up the steps and put his arms around her. "It's good to see you, Mother."

"Hi, Grandma Kate. It's great to see you again." Nova walked up behind Dayton and found herself in her grandmother's arms before she could say anything else.

"Nova, honey. You're so grown up! And even prettier than I imagined! Of course, I always knew you'd be pretty. You were such a beautiful baby."

"Thanks." Nova blushed. "I look like my mom."

"I don't know..." Kate smiled. "I think there's definitely some Grant in there too. You remind me of my mother."

"I do?" Nova felt oddly pleased by the comment. She'd always wanted to look like a Grant.

"Come on in, you two. I have lunch ready." Kate motioned for them to follow her through the front door into the house.

Nova noticed that the door was a much brighter red close up. Maybe her grandmother had a little of the Grant playfulness after all. So far she seemed friendly and welcoming, but Dayton still wore a sober expression.

"Give her a chance, Dad," Nova whispered as the door closed behind them.

Once inside, Kate gave Nova a quick tour of the downstairs. To the left was a music room with a World War Two-era piano. She explained that after the stock market crash of 1929, piano makers had to find cheaper materials for pianos and, for the most part, used plastic instead of the more expensive ivory. Then with the onset of the war, materials used in pianos had been especially hard to come by, as so many resources went into the war effort.

"I bought this piano when I got my first job," she said proudly. "I paid for it myself, every penny. I used to tell Day that he couldn't bang on it because it was a special piano and had to be treated as such." She winked.

"I remember." Dayton finally smiled, but it seemed a little stiff and forced. "I spent hours in the corner for hitting the keys too hard."

"Don't you believe him, Nova! He could be a handful, but I was always a pushover with your dad." Kate looked at Dayton with misty eyes, and it seemed to Nova that she was hoping for confirmation from her son.

After an awkward silence, Dayton finally spoke up. "I guess I was a little defiant at times, wasn't I?"

Kate smiled gratefully. "That's water under the bridge, son. It's just good to have you home."

Kate cheerfully continued showing them the house. Across from the music room was a parlor furnished with an antique settee and chairs. While it was an elegant room, it wasn't inviting. So far, that could be said for Grandma Kate's residence in general, from the overgrown driveway to the immaculate formal rooms—uninviting. This was a home without warmth. Nova felt a wave of sadness for her grandmother and impulsively put her arm around Kate's shoulder as they walked. Kate was so taken by the gesture that she looked for a moment as though she'd break down before she managed to collect herself.

They continued into an elegant dining room. It wouldn't have looked out of place for there to be metal stands and a velvet rope allowing visitors to view the room without disturbing it. Nova wondered if anyone had ever actually eaten in there.

They passed through a butler's pantry into the kitchen. It was tiny in comparison to the one at Willow Hill, but finally there was a room that gave off a warm and friendly feeling. The glass-front cabinets were painted a soft white in contrast to the same rich wood floor that extended throughout the house. There was a cozy table laid out with a red-checked tablecloth and white dishes with a vase full of daisies in the middle. Grandma Kate had something that smelled delicious cooking in a Dutch oven on top of the stove.

"Day, you want to show Nova around upstairs while I put lunch on the table?" Kate asked, already taking bowls out of the cupboard.

"Sure." He seemed glad to get away and headed for the stairs.

As soon as they were out of earshot, Nova said, "She seems really sweet. Why are you acting so weird?"

"I don't know. Maybe because she should be dead and I'm still adjusting to the fact that she's not. Besides, you don't know her like I do. As soon as we start talking about traveling, her attitude will change. Trust me."

"Well, if you don't lighten up, it's probably gonna happen sooner than that."

"Fine. I'll try." At the top of the stairs, Dayton led her down a short hallway and up another short staircase. "I'll show you my room first."

"In the attic?"

"It's not really an attic. You don't notice it from the front of the house, but there's a third-floor room with a big window that overlooks the backyard. I begged for that room until I was eight. That's when she let me move up there. She didn't like me being on a separate floor, so she moved her bedroom to the small one beside the stairs so she could hear me if I needed her. I thought it was silly at the time. Her room was so much bigger, with a huge fireplace and its own bathroom. I guess I understand a little more now. She was probably always worried something would happen to me." He stopped at the landing and turned to Nova. "You're right, firefly. I need to try harder with her. I couldn't relate to her at all when I was young, but now..." He shook his head. "I don't know. I wish I'd been more understanding."

"You were young. I'm sure she realizes that."

Dayton still didn't move, obviously engrossed in the past.

Nova put her hand on his arm. "Show me your room, Dad."

Dayton snapped back to the present and strode over to door just off the landing. When they stepped inside the room, Dayton gasped. "She hasn't changed a thing! It's just like it was when I moved out to go to college. I mean, it looks *exactly* the same! I came home on holidays and during the summer, and I guess it hadn't changed then too, but that makes more sense. I was in college and lots of parents keep their kids' rooms the same while they're school. But this… I don't think I came up here when we visited when you were little. I can't remember." Dayton frowned, apparently trying to picture how his room had looked then. "We stayed in the guest room downstairs on the other side of the house. At least, I think we did. I don't really know what happened in this timeline." He shook his head. "All these years… it's like I never left."

"It's sweet. She missed you."

"I guess she did." His voice sounded strange.

"It looks like she keeps it clean too. I don't see any dust." Nova scanned the room, trying to picture her dad living here as a kid.

There was a double bed with a headboard that looked like a ship's wheel. It didn't really seem like something her dad would have wanted, but she didn't say so. There were two nightstands with lamps made from driftwood. The nautical theme carried through the rest of the room, with one wall painted to look like the ocean and a dresser sporting a large model ship.

"Uh… Dad?"

"Don't say it. I know what you're thinking. Let's just say that when I was eight, I wanted to be a pirate. My mom humored me."

"Yeah, but…"

"Why didn't I change it when I got older?"

She laughed. "I guess."

"I don't know. I didn't think I'd ever come back after I left for college, so I didn't bother. Mother and I never got along that well. I always resented not knowing the family. I blamed her. I know how that must have made her feel, but I couldn't help it. I always thought she should have done something about my dad, you know… changed what happened. I couldn't wait to get out of here. I guess some things don't change, no matter how many times you switch."

"You're not a kid anymore. It's time to get over it. She's your mom."

"I know. Let's go talk to her."

CHAPTER 10

They hurried back downstairs and found Kate spooning vegetable beef soup into ceramic bowls.

"You two can wash up down the hall. I have soup and cornbread for lunch. I hope that suits." She smiled, obviously enjoying the company.

Nova wondered what it was normally like around here, her grandmother in this big house all alone, eating meals at the kitchen table by herself. It must be terribly lonely. What did she do all day long—other than wipe down all the furniture and baseboards, which she apparently did regularly as there didn't appear to be a speck of dust on anything?

They turned to head down the hall to the powder room, but Dayton hesitated, looking back at Kate. "It smells great, Mom."

She seemed instantly close to tears and stirred the soup vigorously, dabbing her eyes with a hand towel. Dayton stood there a moment, watching her as though he wanted to say something else, but he finally turned and led Nova down the hall to the powder room. When they'd washed their hands and returned to the kitchen, Kate handed over to Nova the task of buttering and serving the cornbread.

"This looks so good, Grandma Kate," Nova said sincerely. The bowl of cereal she'd had that morning was long gone and she was starving.

They sat at the table and started eating before Kate cleared her throat and said a short blessing.

"Sorry, Mom. I forgot." Dayton said sheepishly.

"Why should anything be different just because you're grown?" Kate laughed. "I always had trouble getting your dad to take even a few seconds to say a blessing when he was growing up. He was always hungry. I thought he'd eat me out of house and home!"

"Well, Grandma, nothing much has changed." Nova grinned.

"Hey now. How about sticking up for your old man?" Dayton pretended to be wounded.

"You turned out all right, Day." Kate patted his hand. "I'm so glad you decided to come see me. It's been too long. Why didn't Marshall come with you?"

Nova and Dayton choked on their soup at the same time.

"Wha… what did you say?" Dayton managed, still holding his spoon mid air.

"I said why didn't you bring Marshall?"

All the color drained from his face. "Mom… you mean Alana."

"Grandma, you know about Marshall?" Nova gripped the table, steadying herself.

"What's the matter with both of you? Of course I know about Marshall, though no thanks to you, Day!" Kate was suddenly angry. "It would have been nice to see my own grandson at least once!"

"But… how? Alana is…" Dayton couldn't seem to get anything out. He finally gave Nova a look that clearly said *help.*

"Grandma, Marshall—he isn't here."

"Well, I can see that! What are you trying to tell me?" Kate was clearly alarmed. "Did something happen to him?"

Nova took a deep breath. "We went to see Aunt Jean to find out how to… I mean, we wanted to save Alana. You know Alana, right?"

"Well… yes." Kate seemed confused.

"Okay," Nova continued. "In that timeline, the one we were in *then,* we went to Willow because she was—I mean, she had a heart condition and when she was born, they didn't know."

"She died," Kate stated matter-of-factly. "I know all of this." Kate turned to Dayton, glaring. "You took Nova to see my sister? After I expressly forbade it?"

"That was a long time ago, and I'm forty years old! I can do what I damn well please!" Dayton's face was bright red. "And how can you remember Marshall? He wasn't born in this timeline! *Alana* is alive in this life. Why don't you know that? We're all supposed to know when things *change.*"

"Alana is alive?" Grandma Kate looked confused. "Wait… I remember the twins." She appeared to be struggling. "Yes, I know Alana didn't die. You asked me to help you before but not in this life. And Marshall… he was in the last one too, wasn't he? I've been away from all of this so long. It's hard to keep them straight."

"Mom…" Dayton's tone had softened considerably. "When Nova traveled at Aunt Jean's, she switched to a timeline where Alana lived. She's back at home with Celeste right now. But in this reality, we never had Marshall. He's just a memory from a previous life. Nova and I need help getting him back. That's why we came. Can you tell us what to do?"

"*That's* why you came to see me after all these years? So I'd help you travel? Why don't you ask my sister again? She seems to know everything," she said bitterly.

"Mom, Aunt Jean is dead." Dayton was clearly concerned. "Don't you remember? You said something about it when you left me a message."

Kate sat perfectly still, her eyes closed. After a few moments, she opened them again. "I'm sorry. Of course I know Jeannie is dead. And I know where we are now. You don't know what it's like to get jerked from timeline to timeline your whole life, never the one doing it. It's hard to remember which one you're in. They get blurry sometimes. Jeannie should have told you that."

"Mom," Dayton said softly, leaning forward, "we need your help. You remember Marshall. You're the only one who does besides Nova and me."

Nova spoke up. "Grandma, is there anything you can think of that would help us change back to the reality we were in before I traveled?"

Dayton gasped. "What are you saying? You want to go back to that timeline? Alana was dead in that one."

"But Marshall wasn't," Nova said, trying to keep her voice steady. "I want to go back and start over. Try it again. I'll think of *everyone* next time. I'll make sure they're all there."

Kate directed her comment at her son. "Day, what have I told you before? There's nothing you can do. Don't you see? Every time you try to change things, it just gets worse. You might fix one problem only to have three more. If I tried to help you and you lost another child, you'd blame me."

"We'd be careful, Mom."

"It wouldn't matter. It's not in your control. Besides, I haven't even thought about traveling for many years. Not since… it doesn't matter. There's nothing you can do."

"I don't accept that!" Nova spoke up again. "Marshall's not gonna be some character in a picture painted from memory, like the one in the attic at Willow Hill!"

Kate's mouth dropped open. "What are you talking about?"

"Aunt Jean painted a picture of you, Daniel, and Danny Jr. She wanted to remember them because they mattered! She said you wouldn't let the family help you when you lost them. What did they want to do? Could they have brought them back?"

"No! No one could have done anything to change my mistake. I can't believe my sister told you about Daniel. She had no right to do that!" Kate pushed her chair back and paced. "Meddling in my business. That's what she always did. You think I wouldn't have done anything to have my family back? I'm telling you nothing could be done."

"How do you know? You never let them try." Nova tried to stay calm but felt herself on the verge of losing it.

Kate sat down again, her eyes brimming with tears and all of her anger gone. "No, I didn't let them try. Maybe I should have. I was so devastated. I thought I hated all of them. I blamed them for Daniel's death. I was just hiding from the fact that it was my fault. Then it was too late. My parents sent me to Charleston for a new start. That's when I met Sheldon. He was my chance for a normal life away from the family... away from travelers."

"But didn't you stay with relatives in Charleston? Weren't they travelers too?" Dayton asked.

"No, they weren't Grants. They were Mitchells, my grandmother's side of the family. I stayed with my Uncle Brack and his wife, Mary Jane. They had three sons. Brack Jr. was six years older than me. Nate was two or three years younger than him, and George was a year behind me. The boys were kind of wild, always getting into some kind of trouble, but never anything serious. And they were so funny. We laughed all the time. They were a great distraction from all the pain I'd been in since the accident. After I'd been there about a month, Sheldon came to visit." Kate's eyes misted over. "He and Brack Jr. had been best friends since grade school. Sheldon's parents died when he was a boy— influenza, I think. That's why he became a doctor. He lived with the Mitchells all through school. They were like his second family."

"You never told me any of this." Dayton looked mesmerized.

"It's a painful memory. I tried not to think about them... or Sheldon. Your father was a good man. You'd have been so proud of him. He spent his short life trying to help people."

"I know." Dayton put his hand on her shoulder. "Why didn't I ever meet the Mitchells?"

"They were wonderful people. I always meant to take you to Charleston, but after Sheldon died, I just couldn't. I guess I did a pretty good job of cutting you off from everyone who cared about us, didn't I, son?"

"It's okay, Mom. We can still make some things right."

"You mean Marshall, don't you?" Kate frowned. "I told you. There's nothing I can do."

"You won't even think about it? Maybe you'll remember something."

"No." Kate pushed her chair back again and collected the dishes from the table. "You and Nova should come back in the fall. I have maple trees all over the property, and they turn a brilliant gold. Nova and Alana can come up for the pumpkin festival in October too. The young people in town have a pumpkin carving contest and it gets pretty competitive." She continued to prattle on, clearly intending to be done with any talk of traveling.

Nova pushed her chair back and stood. "I need to get some air."

Ignoring them, she went outside and sat in one of the rockers on the front porch, trying to calm down. Their visit wasn't going at all as she had planned. Her dad was right—Grandma Kate seemed determined not to help them. Her stubborn refusal to get involved because of something that happened over forty years ago was infuriating.

From an open window, Dayton's voice cut through her thoughts. He and Kate were apparently in a heated argument in the kitchen. After a few minutes, it seemed to settle down, and Nova hoped he was making some progress. She strained to hear, but their voices were too low.

After a while, Dayton came out to the porch and sat down beside her. "It's no good with your grandmother. Even if she was willing, I don't think there's anything she could do. It's been too long since she even thought about traveling."

"I heard you arguing," Nova said.

"I shouldn't have raised my voice. She seems... confused. Why did she initially think Marshall was alive? It's like she's drifting between timelines, which is strange on several levels. You think her reality and ours aren't in sync?"

"I don't see how that would be possible, but then, none of this should be possible." Nova shook her head. How could they hope to find logical rules for something like time travel?

"Right. So you think that maybe she *is* in both timelines at once?" Dayton asked hopefully.

"No, I don't. Aunt Jean said that other travelers remember the previous timelines even if they aren't the ones who traveled. She said it's like a dream, but you never forget the people you knew. I think Grandma Kate just remembers and can't tell which life is real."

"Maybe. Anyway, it seems we're not getting any help from her, so what's our next step?" Dayton was clearly looking to Nova for a plan.

She felt utterly defeated. "I don't know what we're gonna do."

"You'll think of something."

"Why is it up to me?" Nova asked, frustrated.

"It's not. I'm sorry, firefly. I just thought... never mind. We'll figure it out together, okay?"

"Sure." Nova wished she believed it. "Where's Grandma Kate?"

"She went upstairs. I know she's upset. I should probably go in there and tell her it's okay, but I don't understand her. I know she heard things when she was younger. She had years of being around traveling, even if she wasn't the one doing it." Dayton stood and paced around the porch, working himself up. "She wouldn't even try to save my father, and that should have been possible, even easy.

Just go back to the day he left for Africa. It makes no sense to me."

"She's scared," Nova said sadly.

Dayton stopped pacing and looked at her. "I know. Let's at least go inside and say goodbye to her. I don't want to leave it like this, especially since I may never come back."

"Don't say that. She's still your mom. And I don't want to lose any more family."

Dayton didn't respond. He opened the screen door and Nova followed him into the house. Kate was still upstairs, so they trudged up the steps to the second floor. Her bedroom door was closed. They stood in the hallway, deciding what to do. Then Dayton knocked quietly.

"Mother?" He waited, but no sound came from within. "Mom, we're leaving. I'll get back up here to see you soon, okay?"

There was still no answer.

Dayton turned to Nova. "Let's get out of here." He turned and walked down the stairs.

Nova continued to stand outside of her grandmother's room. Finally she tapped lightly on the door. "Grandma? Can I come in?"

She tried the knob, and it opened easily. Kate was sitting in a chair facing the window. Her room was like the rest of the house—immaculate. A crocheted sweater was draped carefully over her shoulders. She looked so small and frail, much older than her years. When Nova walked over to her, she turned, and Nova saw the anguish in her face.

"I know your dad doesn't understand. I just can't help him. He doesn't know how much I'd like to, but everything I touch turns out badly."

"It's okay. Will you promise me something though?"

"Anything, honey."

"If you think of a way, anything at all, will you call me?"

"I won't."

"But if you do? Just try. Please. I miss Marshall so much."

Tears ran down Kate's cheeks. "I know you do. I'm so sorry. Promise me you'll come back anyway… and bring Alana."

Nova hugged her grandmother. "I promise."

As she descended the stairs, Nova wanted to cry too, but she was in a dark place where tears weren't enough.

CHAPTER 11

Nova heard Dayton on the phone in the kitchen as she descended the stairs. He hung up when she entered.

"Who was that?" she asked.

"Michael. He wants me to come back to Willow to sign some papers and go over things."

"He called here?"

"No. I called Aunt Jean's."

"Oh. When does he want you to come?"

"As soon as possible. I'll take you home, then see about flying down there."

"Dad, let's just go now."

"Leave from here? We can't."

"Why not? We packed for several days. We don't need to go home. Let's fly out from here!"

"There's no airport in Frederick. The closest one that flies into Charlotte would be Boston, but we don't have tickets. I don't even know the flight times. And Michael is expecting me in a few days, not today."

"Can't we get tickets at the airport? You could call Michael back and tell him we're coming. We can go straight to Boston from here. Please, Dad? I have a feeling we need to go."

"What do you mean?" Dayton frowned.

"I don't know exactly. But Willow Hill is where I was when I traveled. I really feel like we need to go back. *I* need to go back." Nova was being honest. Going back to

Aunt Jean's just felt *right*. As much as her aunt and uncle had traveled, there might be something there, some clue. The attic was full of family history. "Dad, let's go now. Please."

"I'd have to call your mother."

"Call her. She won't care. She and Alana are too busy planning the trip."

Dayton stood there a moment, thinking, then smiled. "It's only about an hour to Boston."

Nova threw her arms around him. "Thanks, Dad! Should we go say goodbye again to Grandma Kate?"

"No. Let's just go." He grabbed his keys and walked out with Nova right behind him. When all of this was finally settled, she planned to make him straighten things out with his mother.

They drove back through Frederick, stopping to buy gas and pick up soft drinks at the station on the main road out of town. For some reason, Nova felt a sense of excitement that bordered on euphoria. Dayton seemed to be feeling it too. Before long, they were cruising down I-95 South toward Boston, the windows down and music blaring. It was wonderful to take a break from all the anxiety and worry and just let go of the pent-up emotions.

They breezed on toward Boston, singing at the top of their lungs and laughing about the funny looks they got from other drivers on the road. Nova thought about all the times her family had done this kind of thing in her first timeline, before Dayton was killed. But even then, Celeste had been more reserved than she was now. It made sense that this version of her would be the happiest, since as far as she knew she'd never lost a child. She had twin girls and a husband who was a best-selling author. Her life was good. She was happy in a way that Nova had never seen. *I hope I can keep you that way, Mom.*

The closer they got to the airport, the more excited Nova became, certain that this was the right choice, the one that would make all the difference. Secretly, she knew exactly what she was going to do. She couldn't believe she hadn't thought of it sooner but guessed it was like the old saying her English teacher, Mrs. Chandler, loved to use: "You all can't see the forest for the trees." Nova finally saw the forest. There was really only one person who would know what to do.

They drove straight to Logan International Airport and parked in the extended stay lot. After taking a shuttle to the terminal, they stood in a long line to buy tickets, managing to get a departure time just two hours away. The euphoria of the drive down wore off a little as they made their way through security and found their gate.

"There's no need to sit here and wait. Are you hungry?" Dayton asked.

"I'm starving. We kind of cut lunch short at Grandma's," Nova answered.

"The sign we just passed said there's a barbeque place on this concourse. Let's check it out."

There was a long line at that restaurant, so they picked up sandwiches at a café a few shops down and sat in the corner, away from the other customers. As Nova took a bite of her turkey on rye, she glanced at her dad and noticed that he hadn't even unwrapped his sandwich. He was watching her, obviously with something on his mind.

"What's up?" Nova asked.

"I was thinking about Michael." He kept his voice down even though no one could have heard them over the noisy hustle and bustle of the concourse. "When Aunt Jean talked to me about him, I was probably no more than eight years old. Michael is two or three years younger than me, so the oldest he could have been was six. When my mother and Aunt Jean had their big fight that summer, I remember Jean saying something about there being no set age that the ability comes on. My mother was insisting that I didn't have it, but Aunt Jean was saying I could be a late bloomer, or I hadn't developed it because I hadn't been exposed to traveling. I think my mother was hoping I didn't possess the gift."

"So what are you saying?" Nova asked.

"I'm saying that if I became a traveler after my eighth birthday, then Michael could have been a late bloomer as well. If he was, we may have more help than we thought."

Nova's face lit up. "We need to ask him! Maybe that's how he became so successful. I saw a picture of his family at Aunt Jean's, and they were on vacation somewhere tropical."

"Lots of people are successful. Maybe he did it the old-fashioned way—education and hard work."

"Or maybe he won the lottery. You never know." Nova grinned. "Either way, we have to find out."

"Agreed. But we need to be careful. We can't just come up to him and say, 'Hey Michael, are you a time traveler like the rest of the Grants?' If he's not, he'll think we've lost our minds."

"Yeah… but even if he can't travel, wouldn't he at least know about it? I mean, how could he grow up with Uncle Bill and not know?" Nova pointed out.

"I can't say one way or another. But I can tell you that the Grants have done a pretty good job of keeping it a secret from non-travelers, even close family. So it's entirely possible he wouldn't have a clue. I don't think Aunt Georgia ever knew. I said something around her when I was a kid and Uncle Bill took me aside and gave me a good talking to. Let's tread lightly as far as Michael is concerned. He knows I'm a Grant. If he's a traveler, he may bring it up."

"Okay, I'll be subtle. It would really suck for him if he can't travel though, huh? I mean, being one of the only Grants who can't do it. And what about his kids? What if Michael can't travel but one of his kids can? How would that work?"

"I don't know. I guess if Uncle Bill or Aunt Jean recognized that one of the kids had the gift, they'd have told Michael."

"Yes, but if it happened after they were both gone, would the kid who could travel just never know? Or would he travel accidentally like you did when you had the wreck and find himself in a different reality? I can tell you from personal experience that would seriously freak him out. He'd probably act crazy and that's what his new timeline parents would think he was—crazy."

"Can we deal with our problem before we tackle someone else's?" Dayton asked, shaking his head.

"Sure." Nova giggled. "But, like I said, if he's one of the only Grants who can't travel, it sucks for him."

"Yeah. It sucks, and not just for him. We need all the help we can get." Dayton glanced at his watch. "Time to go. I want to make sure we have a spot in the overhead bins for our bags. It's a full flight."

They arrived at the gate just as the plane was starting to board. Realizing that Michael didn't know they were coming, Dayton dashed off to call him. By the time he got back, they were the last two to board. They had managed to get two seats together, but they were in the back of the plane and the flight attendant had to store their bags somewhere up front. Once that was sorted out, they settled in, relieved to be on their way.

Even though Aunt Jean wouldn't be there, Nova still felt strangely comforted by the fact that they were going back to Willow Hill. She had an idea that she didn't intend to share with her dad. Better to just do it without interference. As much as he wanted to save Marshall, Nova knew that when it came down to it, he'd hesitate to do whatever it took. He was more like his mother than he realized. In the end, it would be up to Nova. She could almost hear her aunt's voice. "Whatever happens, I want you to know I have faith in you."

Nova closed her eyes and smiled. She couldn't wait to talk to her again.

CHAPTER 12

The flight to Charlotte would take about two and a half hours, and Nova planned to spend most of the time trying to remember everything her aunt had told her about traveling. Dayton closed his eyes and leaned his head back as though he was dozing off, but Nova wondered if that was just a way to keep from talking so he could gather his own thoughts.

About fifteen minutes into the flight, the attendant came by with a cart to see if they wanted anything.

"I'm Ashlie. Thank you for choosing to fly with us! Is there anything I can do for you? We have soft drinks, coffee, and snacks. Just pretzels or crackers. Would you like something?" She smiled eagerly.

Ashlie looked very new to the job, no older than twenty. Maybe this was her first flight and that's why she was being so excessively attentive. The other two attendants working the front of the cabin were older and seemed less amiable. Nova sensed that Ashlie would be disappointed if she didn't want anything, so she took a Coke and the tiniest bag of pretzels she'd ever seen.

"I know. There's probably only two or three in there." Ashlie giggled, referring to the pitifully small bag.

"It's okay." Nova smiled. "I'm not that hungry. We just ate."

"Is that your dad? Should I leave something for him too?" Ashlie asked.

"The same, I guess." Nova was anxious for the attendant to move on so she could get back to her thoughts.

Ashlie poured a Coke for Dayton and handed it to Nova. "Your dad looks familiar. Is he famous or something?"

"He's a science fiction writer. Some of his books—"

"Oh my God, is he Dayton Grant? I have all his books!" Ashlie looked as if she wanted to jump up and down but was trying to contain herself.

One of the older flight attendants looked back at her sternly.

"I'm sorry!" Ashlie whispered. "I just can't believe Dayton Grant is on this flight! He's my favorite author! I love his books!"

"Would you like him to sign something?" Nova asked, regretting it almost immediately when it appeared that Ashlie was on the verge of an out-of-body experience.

"Do you think he would? That would be the best thing that's ever happened to me!"

"I certainly hope not," Nova muttered under her breath. She nudged Dayton. "Dad. Wake up."

Dayton opened his eyes, slightly startled that the flight attendant was shoving an emergency instruction manual in his face.

"Mr. Grant, it's an honor to meet you! I've read all your books!"

"Oh… great, uh… are you sure it's okay to sign this?"

"Oh, we have lots of them." She giggled. "That's Ashlie with an 'ie' not a 'y.'"

One of the other attendants was making his way down the aisle toward them with a smoldering expression. He arrived just as Dayton handed the autographed manual back to the young attendant.

"Sir, let me apologize —"

"Nothing at all to apologize for," Dayton interrupted. "I'd like to thank you for assigning this friendly young lady to our section. You don't often see flight attendants so thoughtful and eager to make sure the customer has a comfortable flight. I hope you pass along my compliment to the captain.”

“Well, of course… um… good job, Ashlie,” he sputtered, obviously flustered.

“My dad’s a best-selling author,” Nova chimed in, grinning.

Dayton shot her an amused look.

“Well… yes. It’s a pleasure to have you aboard, sir.”

“Thank you. If we need anything, we’ll let Ashlie know,” Dayton said, clearly dismissing the senior attendant.

“Very good. Carry on, Ashlie.” He took off up the aisle to the safety of his own section and didn’t look their way again.

“That was awesome!” Ashlie giggled. “I’ve never seen Robert that flustered! You two just let me know if you want anything at all.”

“We will,” Dayton assured her.

“Back in a bit.” She smiled as she continued up the aisle, forcing soft drinks and pretzels on other passengers.

Nova smiled at Dayton. “You’re pretty cool, Dad.”

He laughed. “Yeah, I have my moments. ‘My dad’s a bestselling author,’” he repeated, mimicking her, then chuckled.

“Just doing my part.” Nova grinned.

Nova downed her Coke in less than a minute. *Okay, Ashlie, I admit it. That was refreshing.* She looked at Dayton to say something, but he seemed to have dozed off again. Leaning her head back against the seat, Nova let her mind go into overdrive, not realizing how much time had passed until Ashlie reappeared to collect the cups.

“We’re getting ready to land, so I have to get these… unless you want to hold them. We have to push the tray tables up.” Ashlie looked at Dayton’s Coke, still sitting on his tray. “Do you want to save that?” she asked, clearly disappointed.

Dayton opened his eyes. “No need.” He chugged the

whole thing down and handed her the cup.

She looked as if she was about to swoon. As she continued up the aisle, Nova noticed that she stuck his cup in her pocket instead of throwing it away.

"Is this what it's like at all those book signings you do?" Nova asked, thoroughly impressed. "Rabid fans asking for autographs and saving your plastic cups?"

"Of course not." Dayton grinned. "Sometimes the cups are Styrofoam."

"Seriously? Oh my God." Nova shook her head, laughing.

"Just don't order me a soft drink next time. How do you drink that stuff?"

"Acquired taste," she answered.

"Must be. So what did you do while I was unconscious?"

"I just sat here thinking about Marshall."

That was only a half-truth. She had been thinking about Marshall, but mostly she had been going over every conversation she'd had with her aunt, in as much detail as possible. To her, it had only been a few days since she'd talked with Aunt Jean, so it wasn't hard to recall their conversations. Only a few days, and so much had changed. Nova had learned a valuable lesson—traveling should never be taken lightly, because your whole life could change in a heartbeat. She'd be more careful next time.

Dayton squeezed her hand. "I know, firefly. We'll figure this out."

It was seven fifteen by the time they landed in Charlotte, disembarked, and made their way through the terminal. Michael had told Dayton he'd be there at seven forty-five, so they waited in a coffee shop just off the main hub.

"Do you want anything?" Dayton asked absently.

"Not really."

Dayton eyed her suspiciously. "You're planning something, aren't you? Seriously, since we landed, you've been preoccupied. What are you up to?”

“Nothing. I’ve just been thinking about Grandma Kate,” Nova lied.

“That’s it?”

“Yeah, that’s it. I hate the way we left things with her.”

“Don’t worry about my mother. We’ll make up later. Right now, I want to concentrate on Marshall.”

“Me too.”

“And we’d better eat something. It’s getting late, and Aunt Jean’s not there with an incredible meal waiting for us.”

He seemed to regret his remark as soon as he said it, but Nova had been thinking the same thing. Aunt Jean was the most amazing woman she’d ever met. Willow Hill would seem empty without her.

There was a burger bar next to the coffee shop, so Dayton bought them a couple of hamburgers while Nova waited at their table. When they were finished eating, they took the escalator to the bottom level where baggage claim was located.

Something occurred to Nova as they were riding down. “How are you gonna recognize Michael?”

“I thought about that,” Dayton answered. “From what I remember, he looks a lot like Uncle Bill. Over the years, I’ve seen the occasional photo and you saw the picture at Aunt Jean’s. Between the two of us, I guess we’ll figure it out.”

As it turned out, they didn’t need to recognize him. Michael was waiting outside in a dark blue BMW. When he spotted them, he jumped out and waved, striding forward to meet them. Dayton seemed relieved and shook Michael’s hand before grabbing their bags.

“Thanks for picking us up. Sorry for the last minute notice,” Dayton said.

“No problem at all!” Michael seemed genuinely pleased. “I appreciate you coming so soon. My girls have a dance recital in three days. My wife called this morning asking if I was going to be there. If we can wrap this up quickly, I can still make it! You know how it is."

"Yes, I do." Dayton smiled, winking at Nova.

They loaded into the car and set out for Willow with Nova in the backseat. The ride had been part of the adventure the last time they'd come. Nova had loved the journey from city to countryside, passing planted fields and the house with the tire swing. It had all been exciting. This time was different. This time she had one thing on her mind.

When they reached Willow, Nova was glad to be in the backseat so Michael and her dad couldn't see that she was fighting to stay together. In the waning light, most of the establishments were dark. Aunt Jean had said that Willow rolled up the sidewalks at night, and it was practically true. There were only two couples strolling along, one walking a dog and the other couple holding hands and talking. It wasn't the lively place, bustling with families, it had been when they drove through the first time.

And Aunt Jean wouldn't be there when they reached Willow Hill. She wouldn't be standing on the porch in her yellow shirt and riding boots, so happy to see them. There wouldn't be mounds of food waiting for them on the massive kitchen table. Marshall wouldn't be running down to the barn to help Justin, begging for a horse of his own. Celeste wouldn't be there, throwing herself into helping to get the nursery ready for Justin and Connie's baby. Every single thing that made Willow Hill special would be gone. Nova felt tears running down her cheeks and wiped them off quickly.

She knew exactly what she'd say when she saw Aunt Jean. *Why did you have to die? I need you.*

They turned onto the road that would take them to Willow Hill. When they arrived, Nova looked out the window at the stately entrance. The house loomed ahead, huge and quiet. Michael pulled the car around the circle at the end of the driveway and let Nova and Dayton out.

"I'm going to run down to the barn quickly. I need to pick up some papers from Justin. Just make yourselves at home."

They carried their bags in through the front door and stopped, looking around.

"It seems empty, doesn't it?" Dayton observed. "It's amazing how one person made this house seem so full."

"I know," Nova said sadly. "I was thinking that too."

"Same rooms?"

"Sure."

She started up the steps with her dad behind her. At the top, Nova turned right and headed down the hallway to her room. When she stepped inside, everything was as she remembered it, except it smelled a little musty and there was a thin layer of dust on the wood furniture. She dropped her bag on the floor beside the window seat and opened the window. The smell of flowers drifted in, comforting her a little.

Though it was getting dark outside, from the veranda lights, Nova could see that the garden already looked overgrown. After all, it had been a month since Aunt Jean had passed away. Most likely, the estate had let the gardeners go, and Justin probably had too much to do at the barn to pay attention to the garden. Nova pictured it the way it had looked when she and Dayton had walked down the path and talked to Aunt Jean for the first time about traveling. In reality that had been less than a week ago, but it felt much longer, almost as if it had never happened.

From her window, Nova could make out the top of the gazebo in the waning light. She could picture herself sitting in one of the wicker chairs, hanging on Aunt Jean's every word. She closed her eyes for a moment and replayed the scene in her head. She'd give almost anything to be back there. If she had the chance to do it all over again, she wouldn't dive headfirst into a power she hadn't learned to fully control. She'd bide her time, making sure she was ready, that she'd thought of everything and everyone.

Nova was still gazing out the window when Michael tapped on her open door and stepped inside.

"I meant to tell you… Aunt Jean left you that chest of drawers. It was the only thing specifically named in the will. Was it special to you?"

"Not really," she answered, confused. "I stayed in this room when I was here before, but I don't remember ever talking about the chest. I have no idea why she left it to me."

Once again, Nova realized she'd spoken too soon. What if, in this timeline, she hadn't stayed in this room before? Of course, how would Michael know if she had or not? Still, she needed to be more careful.

"Well, Aunt Jean had her own mind, so I'm sure she had a reason. Anyway, we can arrange to ship it to you."

"Okay, thanks."

Michael turned to leave, but Nova stopped him. "I wanted to ask you something." She tried to figure out the best way to phrase the question. "Did you ever, I mean—" Nova decided to go for it. "Michael, what do you know about time travel?"

Michael stared at her with an amused expression. "Well, you're a Grant all right!" He laughed. "What is it with time travel and this family?"

"It's amazing, isn't it?" Nova responded excitedly.

"I guess you get your interest in science fiction naturally. I never found the subject appealing, but Dad and Aunt Jean used to talk about that stuff sometimes when they thought I wasn't listening. It was almost like they thought it was real." He shook his head, still laughing. "It's paid off pretty well for your dad though. How many best sellers does he have?"

"Five or six, I guess," Nova answered, deflated. Michael wasn't a traveler. "I love my dad's books too.

Maybe some of the things he writes about are true."

"Yeah, well, if you happen to time travel any time soon, give my regards to George Washington."

"Will do." Nova decided to go with the joke and saluted. It didn't matter. He couldn't help and wouldn't believe her if she told him the truth.

Michael nodded. "I'll leave you alone. You look tired. The kitchen is pretty well stocked. Connie's been cooking, and some of Aunt Jean's friends dropped off food since they knew I was here wrapping things up. Help yourself if you get hungry."

"I will," she answered as he retreated down the hall.

Well, I guess that answers that question. She turned and looked at the antique chest. *Now, why did you leave me that, Aunt Jean?*

She walked over and pulled open the top drawer. Empty. She tried every drawer and found the same thing—nothing. Shaking her head, she climbed up on the four-poster bed and lay down, staring at the ceiling. Somewhere in the house, a clock was ticking, the same clock she'd heard the night she traveled. She lay there listening to it for a while, until she couldn't stand it any longer.

Needing a distraction, Nova jumped up and opened the attic door, then climbed the rough stairs without even checking for spider webs. After all she'd been through, it was the spiders who needed to worry. When she pulled the chain attached to the ceiling bulb at the top of the stairs and stepped into the attic, she was relieved to see that nothing had changed, even the creepy doll staring at her from the top shelf to her right.

"You don't scare me," she said to the doll, who continued to observe her with those blank eyes. "Okay, you scare me a little." Nova shivered.

The trunks were in exactly the same places, indicating that no one had come up here in this timeline either. She easily found the one with the paintings and pulled out the picture of Kate and her first family. Studying the child, she realized that he looked remarkably like his dad—dark hair and fine features. Daniel had been a handsome man. She could see why Kate had fallen for him. And Kate was stunning. No wonder he'd been so taken with her.

Nova thought about her grandmother the way she looked now and tried to merge the two images, past and present. She saw the resemblance, but more than the passage of time had changed Kate. She'd had a beautiful family with their whole lives ahead of them and their loss had done something to her. Nova wondered if her grandmother had loved Sheldon as much as Daniel, if she'd felt his loss as keenly. It was understandable that Grandma Kate believed she was cursed. With so much tragedy, who wouldn't think that?

Nova put the painting back in the trunk and looked around the attic. There was a lot to take in. The place was full of antique furniture, toys, books, and too many other items to list. The shelves that lined the wall opposite the door were stuffed with books. Nova browsed through the collection, surprised to find that they were mostly journals, ledgers, and history books.

Nova pulled one of the journals off the shelf and a fine cloud of dust floated up, making her cough violently. She flipped through the pages, trying not to breathe in too deeply lest she suffer another coughing fit. As she read the entries, she realized that this was a child's journal. Most of the entries were about adventures around the farm. Some of them were certainly imaginary, as Nova felt sure that Willow Hill had never been attacked by pirates. She carefully replaced the book, trying not to stir up any more dust.

The first page in the next book talked about an accident. The author's parents had been killed in a car wreck and he talked about missing them. He questioned why it had happened and mentioned a girl who visited him in the hospital. Nova flipped to the inside cover and saw the name Justin Hayes. She quickly shut the book and put it back on the shelf, ashamed that she had intruded on what was obviously Justin's private journal, written shortly after his parents' accident.

Nova walked around the perimeter of the attic, taking in the thousands of items crammed on the floor-to-ceiling shelves. There appeared to be no order to the chaos, no system with which to keep track of things. Nova had the thought that Dayton must have come by his utter lack of organization naturally. Celeste had always called his office "the black hole" because things that went in rarely came out. That was why she kept her personal papers under the bed in her room.

Nova did another sweep of the attic. It must have taken many years to amass such a collection of random things. Nova wondered why Aunt Jean and Uncle Bill had kept it all. There must have been a hundred mason jars. What possible purpose did that many have? Next to the jars sat an old-fashioned typewriter. She tapped one of the dusty keys and it hit the roller with a surprisingly loud click.

"Are you up there, firefly?" Dayton called from her room.

Nova jumped, startled. "Yes, Dad. I'll be right down."

She turned to leave but paused at the trunk where she'd found the coins. When she pulled open the lid, she was pleased to see they were still there.

"I need a good luck charm," she whispered to the guard doll on her perch overhead. After quietly extracting an old coin from the bag, she shoved it into the pocket of her jeans and closed the lid.

Dayton appeared at the attic door. "I wondered where you were. Wow, look at all this stuff. No wonder Michael said Aunt Jean didn't throw anything away. It would take weeks to make a dent in this place."

"Maybe we won't have to. Besides, I feel funny getting rid of any of Aunt Jean's things, don't you?"

"I do. Whatever happens, maybe we'll just leave everything as it is. Aunt Jean left us the house and everything in it, but she asked in her will that we let Michael take some things that remind him of Uncle Bill."

"She didn't leave anything to Michael?"

"Not anything tangible. It was his choice. But she left him financially set for life whether he works or not. It's been a shock to see how much wealth Aunt Jean, Uncle Bill, and

Aunt Georgia accumulated." He shook his head. "Michael lives in Dallas and has a vacation home in Maui. He doesn't need or want the farm."

"So we really are the only poor members of the Grant family." Nova laughed.

"We're not poor," her dad replied sternly. "Just because we're not rich like the rest of the family doesn't mean we're destitute. I've done pretty well as a writer, and we have a nice home in Connecticut. That's more than a lot of people can say."

"I know. I was kidding," Nova said sincerely. "I love our home."

"Me too, honey." He smiled. "Still, it's impressive to see how much Aunt Jean and Uncle Bill accomplished. Did I mention that your aunt also left a small fortune to St. Jude's Children's Hospital in Memphis?"

Nova shook her head.

"They could build a whole new wing if they wanted to. It's pretty impressive. I knew she was well-off, but never had any idea of the magnitude."

"I can't believe this house is ours now."

"Not just the house, honey. She left us the funds to maintain it and then some."

"I guess there are all kinds of ways to get rich if you're able to go back in time," Nova said, imagining some of them. "Like seeing what the lottery numbers are, then going back one day and picking those numbers."

Dayton laughed. "Don't get any ideas, firefly. I'm not sure I want to start playing that kind of game. It seems wrong, like cheating."

"Still, it's pretty cool to think about." She pretended to contemplate that scenario.

"What do you say we go down to the kitchen and see what's what?" He grinned.

"You seem to be in a good mood." Nova smiled.

"I'm glad to be here, I guess." He put his arm around her shoulder. "It's almost like Aunt Jean is here, isn't it? Like she could come walking in any minute?" He had that boyish look on his face, the one she'd come to know over the years that had long ago made her realize her dad was just a big kid.

"I feel it too. She's here somewhere. It's nice that she left us the house and everything, but I'd gladly give it up if..."

"I know, firefly. Me too."

As they left the room, Dayton looked back. "You left the attic door cracked open. Did you mean to do that?"

He walked over and pushed it, but it wouldn't close all the way. A piece of the seal near the floor had come off and was jammed under the door. No matter how hard he pushed, he couldn't get it to click shut.

"Never mind. I'll fix it later," he said.

"Or maybe we'll get Michael to fix it," Nova said. Her dad wasn't very handy. He'd tried to fix a stopped-up sink once, and one ruined kitchen floor later, they'd finally called in a professional.

"Thanks for having so much confidence in your old man." He pretended to be wounded.

"Just saying it like it is, Dad."

As they headed off to the kitchen, she had a vision of the dolls coming though the unlatched door, and a chill ran up her spine. She'd definitely have to get Michael or Justin to fix it!

An hour later, Nova was back in her room, lying on the bed again. Their light mood hadn't lasted long and they'd decided to call it a night. She missed Aunt Jean terribly. Sitting in the kitchen and eating a casserole furnished by a neighbor had made her aunt's absence so conspicuous.

Nova closed her eyes, willing herself to relax. Suddenly, she came to a realization. She sat up, staring at the old chest. Her aunt had a reason for everything. She couldn't have just left it to Nova on a whim. It meant something.

Well, I'll have to ask her when I see her. She smiled. *And there's no time like the present...*

CHAPTER 13

Nova lay back on the bed, took in a deep breath, and let it out slowly. She repeated this process for at least five minutes, until she felt her body relax. She could hear the crickets in the garden and an owl off in the distance. Keeping her breathing steady, she focused on the sound of the clock as she had before. Slowly, the sounds from the garden began to fade, along with everything else. Except the clock. Tick. Tock. Tick. Tock. She would *visit* her aunt. That was what her great-grandmother had called it. She could travel back and return to the same spot as long as she didn't lose the connection. She had no idea how long she'd have, but she'd make sure she left in time to get back to this moment.

Nova focused all of her energy on a picture in her mind—Aunt Jean in the kitchen, preparing something that smelled delicious. Muffins, or maybe cinnamon coffee cake. Nova imagined waking up to that aroma. Her aunt would be humming, like she loved to do when she cooked. She could hear Aunt Jean bustling around and even smell the lilac soap she'd used to wash her hands. Nova imagined waking up and running down the stairs. "Well aren't you a pretty thing!" her aunt would say.

Nova felt herself floating. She continued to focus on Aunt Jean, her voice, her laugh, the sounds and smells of the kitchen early in the morning when the house was still sleeping. Nova floated another few moments in that blissful place, then came the sudden tugging sensation. She could still hear her aunt as she felt herself moving quickly through the tunnel.

A wonderful aroma filled her nostrils—blooming flowers from the garden mixed with sweet cinnamon bread, fresh out of the oven. Nova jolted awake. Sunlight was streaming in through the window and the early birds were chirping in the garden. She shot out of bed and raced down the stairs and into the kitchen, her heart beating furiously. Aunt Jean was pulling a tray of muffins out of the oven.

"My goodness, Nova! You're up early! I thought—"

Before she could get another word out, Nova flew into her arms, nearly burning them both on the hot muffin tray. Her aunt managed to drop it on the counter before grabbing Nova by the shoulders and shoving her back an arm's length.

Staring into her face, Aunt Jean said quietly, "What have you done, child?"

"Aunt—I came back—I had to..." Nova couldn't catch her breath or get her brain to cooperate.

Aunt Jean steered her over to the bench at the table and sat her down. Then she pushed Nova's head down and had her take a couple of deep breaths before letting her up again. "Okay, honey. Slowly. What's going on?"

"Aunt Jean—" Nova took another deep breath and tried to calm down as her head cleared a little. "I tried to call you, get your help. But Michael answered and said you were... we had to meet him here, and I thought about what you said, about visiting." Nova tried to get a hold on her emotions. She wasn't making sense and time was short. She took another breath and started again. "Dad and I came here to meet Michael, to go over the estate. Because..."

"I'm dead," Aunt Jean said quietly.

"Yes." Nova hugged her aunt again, not wanting to let go of her.

"Well, what do you know? It finally happened." She chuckled. "Nova, listen. We have to get down to business. You don't have very long before you'll have to go back.

Close your eyes. You should be able to feel the line between here and where you came from. Can you feel it?"

Nova closed her eyes and concentrated. Amazingly, she could feel the connection to the room upstairs and the time she'd come from. It was like a cord, softly tugging at her, ready to reel her in. Her eyes flew open. "That's incredible!"

"Yes, it is. Now, stay aware of that connection. When you feel it fading, you have to go right then or you'll be stuck."

"Okay, Aunt Jean."

"Now tell me what was so important that you had to risk traveling to talk to me about it."

"It's Marshall. That night, after I practiced traveling with you, I did it again. Only this time, I brought Alana back."

"Did you now?" Aunt Jean's expression turned solemn. "Tell me about that."

"Well, it was so easy traveling in the garden. I thought I could do something bigger. I spent all day planning it in my head, the exact time I'd shoot for—our sixteenth birthdays. After I left you all on the porch that night, I went up to bed and did it. I woke up at home and Alana was alive." Nova's eyes misted over. "It was amazing, Aunt Jean. Having my sister. It took hours for me to realize Marshall was gone."

Aunt Jean was frowning. "Alana was dead before?"

"Yes. She died at birth. Don't you remember?"

"We'll get to that in a minute," her aunt said. "Tell me how you came to be here in the first place."

"We came here to see you, to find out how to travel so we could save Alana. Dad thought you'd be able to help us since you'd offered years ago." Nova was confused. Why was she wasting time going over what her aunt should already know?

"So you and I practiced traveling, then you went back and saved your sister?"

"Yes! Only I did something wrong. I didn't think about Marshall!" Nova started crying. "He's gone. Never born. Just like Grandma Kate's little boy. And it's all my fault. I shouldn't have tried it on my own." Nova decided right then not to tell her aunt that she had helped her. There didn't seem to be any point.

"So you and your family were here visiting me when all of this happened. And that's when I told you about Kate's first family?"

Nova was stunned. "Yes. Don't you remember?"

"How old were you honey?"

"A-almost sixteen."

"You're not now. You just had your fifteenth birthday three days ago. Your parents and Alana are upstairs right now, still asleep. So you're talking about a time that hasn't happened yet and will never happen in this timeline."

Nova stared at her aunt, stunned. She couldn't speak for a minute, then managed weakly, "I'm fifteen? It's last summer?"

"That's right."

Nova flew to the mirror in the hall just outside the kitchen. Sure enough, she looked a little younger, but her hair was still halfway down her back. There was a scratch on her cheek and a small red place on her nose. Nova gingerly touched the spot and it was sore.

Aunt Jean came up behind her. "Let's go back in the kitchen, honey. Our voices may carry upstairs from here."

Nova followed her into the kitchen and sat on the bench at the table, thoroughly shaken.

"We can't let the others know," Aunt Jean cautioned.

Nova felt as if her heart had leapt into her throat. "Am I—upstairs too?"

"No. You're here. There's only one of each of us, honey."

"Thank God." Nova was relieved. The idea of running into another version of herself was terrifying. "So you remember Alana being born? Her heart condition... all of it?"

"Of course I do." Aunt Jean was frowning. "She had surgery when she was still a tiny little thing."

"But Marshall isn't here?"

"No, he's not."

"I guess not," Nova said sadly. "Because I'm still in the same timeline. But you remember him, don't you?"

"I remember that there was a Marshall. He resembled Alana, same hair and eyes. And that smile." She shook her head. "But he doesn't feel exactly… real."

"You told me before that you always remember the people, but the other life feels like a dream."

"That's right. I remember that you had a little brother named Marshall, but not much else. He's just an image really. Do you remember when I told you that eventually you have to stop traveling because it gets harder to focus?"

"I remember."

"Well, honey, it's more than that. When you've traveled a lot, the timelines can get… mixed up. It's like the lines start to blur. You can become confused. It's not safe to travel anymore when that happens because you can't be sure anymore of where you'll end up. The target never fully comes into focus. Focus is key. Without it, you're just shooting in the dark."

"Did that happen to you?"

"It was starting to happen. I couldn't see exactly where I was going anymore, no matter how hard I tried."

"So you couldn't help me even if there was a way, could you?" Nova asked.

"I'm afraid not. Not the way you want me to. I could possibly give you a boost, but that's about it. I'm sorry, honey." Aunt Jean put her arms around Nova and hugged her tightly.

"I talked to Michael. Why isn't he a traveler like you and Uncle Bill?" Nova asked.

"Some just aren't, I'm afraid. We don't know why, but it probably has to do with genes. Bill was so disappointed when he realized that his own son didn't have the gift. He'd dreamed of teaching Michael how to control his ability just like our mother taught us. But by the time Michael was in college, we all knew he'd never have it. It would be up to us to provide for him. By then, we'd switched timelines several times and built up a considerable amount of wealth. No matter how many times we switched, Michael never noticed a thing. Even before you develop the ability yourself, you know something's up when your timeline changes. That's always how it starts. I think Bill went to his grave hoping that someday—"

"He thinks it's science fiction," Nova interrupted.

"Michael?"

"Yeah. I came right out and asked him what he thought about time travel. He heard you and Uncle Bill talking about it when you thought he couldn't hear, but he thought it wasn't real."

"Hmm. He was a sneaky little thing." Jean laughed. "But in the end, I guess we did a pretty good job of keeping him in the dark. Bill never wanted to tell him, and I agreed. I mean, what could he have said? 'Son, most of our family has the ability to travel through time. Unfortunately, you're not one of them.' No, he was right not to tell him. It was hard keeping the secret, but we managed."

"Yeah. I guess it would be better not to know. I wouldn't want to if I was one of the ones who couldn't do it."

"Exactly."

"I guess that's it then."

"I guess so, honey," Aunt Jean said solemnly. "Tell me about Marshall. What was he like?"

"He loved the horses," Nova said sadly. "We couldn't keep him away from the barn. He wanted to take one home with us."

"A little boy after my own heart." Aunt Jean shook her head again. "I wish I remembered that."

"And now Marshall won't ever be here unless you can tell me how to get him back."

"It's not that easy, honey. In this timeline, you don't have a little brother, so no one can go back and save him. You'll have to find another way."

"But how?" Nova cried. "If you can't do it, how can I?"

Aunt Jean closed her eyes, sitting perfectly still. When she opened them again, they were full of tears. "I need time to think about it. Unfortunately, time is something you don't have. The line back to your present time only lasts so long. It's not set in stone. You have to be conscious of it."

Nova couldn't feel the tug now. She was losing the connection. "I can't feel it anymore…"

"Nova, take a breath and concentrate. Is it still there?"

Nova focused on the lifeline back to the present. It was still there, but definitely much weaker. "I feel it a little."

"We have to hurry. You have to go back." She took Nova's arm and steered her into the hallway and toward the steps. "Were you upstairs when you traveled?"

"Yes. In the guest room."

"Go back there. It'll make it easier."

"Wait!" Nova cried. "You left me the old chest of drawers in the guest room. Why did you do that?"

Aunt Jean frowned for a moment, then her face lit up. "The journal! My mother's journal! It'll be in there somewhere, and it might have the answers you're looking for. And I'll do what I can. Now go!"

"You will? How?" Nova clung to her aunt's hand.

"I don't know yet. Just go!"

"Can I come back? I could do it again so we can talk longer!"

"No. Save your strength. I think you're going to need it. But you know where I am if you get desperate. Hurry up, now!"

Nova quickly hugged her aunt then took off up the stairs and down the hall before throwing herself onto the bed. She could hear activity down the hall, so she jumped up and locked the door before climbing back onto the four-poster.

Her brain groped wildly for the line back to the present. *Where is it...? Where is it...?*

Suddenly she felt it, weak but still there. She shut her eyes and listened for the clock, willing herself to block out everything else. Slowly the other sounds around her faded out. Clinging to the slender thread that connected her to the present, she reached out with her mind and grabbed hold of it, almost immediately feeling the familiar sensation of floating.

Right at that moment, someone knocked on the door. "Nova, why is your door locked? Open up! Aunt Jean's down there cooking!"

It was Alana. Nova felt the thread slipping away. It would be easy to just let go, to stay here and experience this year with Alana. A whole year of life with her sister. A year she wouldn't be able to remember otherwise. She could go back for Marshall after that. What difference would it make? Because she'd be back where she started, the summer of her sixteenth year.

The thread had almost withered away to nothing. Nova hesitated another moment before certainty set in. If she waited a year, she wouldn't be back where she started. Everything would be different, and it would be even harder to go back. No, if she gave in to the urge to stay here, Marshall would surely be lost forever. She had to go back.

Nova forced herself to hold on to the connection and tried desperately to shut out her sister's voice. Alana knocked a few more times, then gave up. Nova heard her footsteps down the hall, growing fainter and fainter. She listened again for the clock. The connection to her other timeline was weak.

She willed herself to relax, to focus on the clock as she took slow, deep breaths. Her heart rate slowed a little as she continued the rhythmic breathing. She heard more activity in the hallway outside her door, but now it seemed far away. Finally there were no more sounds. Nothing but the clock. Then it happened again—the sensation of floating. She held on to the fragile connection with all of her will until she felt herself being sucked through the passage, back to where she started, back to the present.

Nova sat up, slightly disoriented. She tried to shake off the fog that had enveloped her. The clock on the night table read 8:52, exactly as it had before she'd traveled. Nova looked at the chest of drawers and shook her head. She'd already looked through all the drawers. They'd been empty. *Okay, Aunt Jean. If you say it's in there, it has to be in there.*

Nova swung her legs over the side of the bed and stood, feeling slightly off-balance. Grabbing one of the bedposts to steady herself, she waited until the dizziness subsided. After a few minutes, she felt normal enough to search the chest again. She began opening the drawers, one by one. They still appeared empty, so she repeated the process, this time pulling each drawer out all the way.

On the next to the last drawer, her luck changed. Taped underneath was a large envelope. Nova pried it loose, opened the clasp, and found a journal with a name printed on the cover in gold leaf—Evelyn G. Grant.

CHAPTER 14

Her hands were shaking when she opened the cover. What was immediately evident was that this was not a traditional journal at all. It was an instruction manual on time travel. Aunt Jean's talk in the garden had been the tip of the iceberg. Evelyn went into more detail, stating that not all travelers possessed equal abilities. Some could travel at will, jumping into other timelines that intersected with their own. She talked about the possibility of using someone else's timeline to change your own trajectory. She also confirmed that one traveler could assist another, like Aunt Jean had done the night Nova brought Alana back.

Evelyn talked about traveling many times over the years. She wrote about training her children to travel and commented that "Jeannie" seemed particularly adept at it, while "Katie" was timid, needing constant encouragement. She felt that "Billy" was too bold, even reckless, and this obviously worried her. Nova relished this new perspective, seeing her grandmother, aunt, and uncle through the eyes of their mother. Maybe it had been Uncle Bill's boldness that had amassed their fortune over the years. Nova couldn't picture Aunt Jean caring about wealth one way or the other.

Nova was so engrossed in her great-grandmother's journal that she didn't notice her dad enter the room. When she looked up and saw him standing there, she nearly jumped out of her skin.

"Don't do that!" she said breathlessly.

"Do what?"

"Sneak up on me."

"You didn't hear me calling you?"

"I guess not." Nova folded down the corner of the page to mark her spot in the journal.

"Why are you still awake?" he asked, yawning. "This wasn't a long enough day? We have an early morning."

"Dad, you have to read this."

"What is it?" he asked, suddenly alert.

"Evelyn's journal. She talks about traveling, and she says you can use someone else's timeline to change yours. It's not real clear how, but I haven't read it all yet."

"Aunt Jean didn't say anything about using someone else's timeline." He was obviously skeptical.

"Maybe she didn't know how to do it. Maybe she hadn't read her mother's journal or just never needed to try it. Or she could have worried that it was too much information at one time for us that day in the garden. When we were here before, we were just learning how to travel. I'm sure Aunt Jean would have shared more if we'd been here longer... if I'd waited."

"I don't know."

"Dad, Evelyn *taught* Aunt Jean. Don't you think we should pay attention if she says you can do something?"

"I guess we should." Dayton thought for a moment. "So whose timeline can we use?"

"Well, since Grandma Kate remembers Marshall, maybe we can use hers."

Dayton was obviously skeptical. "What makes you think she'd agree after what happened at her house this morning? I'm assuming she'd have to be involved."

"I don't know. I need to read the rest of Evelyn's journal, but I think from what I've read so far, Grandma Kate would have to be willing to work with us. The tricky part is that so far, the journal doesn't spell out exactly *how* to do it. It just says you can."

Dayton took the journal from Nova, sat beside her on

the bed, and started reading. After about fifteen minutes, he looked up. "This is amazing."

"I know," Nova responded quietly.

"Where'd you find it?"

"It was in the chest." Nova hesitated, deciding to wait until later to tell him about her *visit* with Aunt Jean.

"Okay, firefly. When we get up in the morning, I'll tell Michael I need to get back, something about my publisher needing me there. We'll take a flight back to Boston late tomorrow. I'll go call right now."

"What about Alana? If she's a traveler, we may need her."

"All right. When we get home, we'll tell her everything."

Nova put her arms around him. "Thanks, Dad. It'll be okay."

"I hope so, honey. Now get some sleep." He kissed the top of her head before leaving the journal with her, walking out, and pulling the door closed.

Feeling as if she'd been up for days, Nova stuck the journal in her overnight bag. She took a quick shower, dried her hair, and climbed in the four-poster. Staring at the ceiling, she remembered the coin in her jeans pocket. She jumped up and retrieved it, placing it on the night table beside her. *Thanks, Aunt Jean,* she thought as she drifted off.

Nova's bare feet against the cool wood made no sound as she descended the stairs. Someone was in the kitchen, shuffling pots and pans and humming an eerily familiar song. For some reason, Nova hesitated, afraid to get any closer. It couldn't be her aunt. She was dead. Feeling a little disoriented, Nova stepped into the kitchen and found Aunt Jean leaning over the granite countertop, rolling out pie pastry.

"Come on, honey, let's get these pies in the oven. I thought we'd practice traveling again while they're baking. Celeste and Connie are in town, and Dayton's at the barn

with Marshall."

"Aunt Jean, how are you here?"

Aunt Jean chuckled. "Now that's the question, isn't it? Let's get this finished before Marshall comes bouncing in and distracts us."

"But, Aunt Jean... I already traveled. Alana's back and Marshall's gone. Don't you remember?"

Nova jolted awake. The sun was streaming through her open window, bringing with it the morning sounds of the garden. Her door was cracked open and she could smell something delicious coming from the kitchen downstairs. She shook her head, trying to clear the dream away, but she could still smell the aroma. Had she traveled back again?

Nova bolted from the bed, grabbed shorts and a shirt from her suitcase, and pulled them on as she ran down the hall to the steps. She hesitated at the top to catch her breath. Someone was frying bacon and bustling around. Descending the stairs quickly, Nova stepped into the kitchen and her heart sank. Connie was standing at the stove, wearing one of Aunt Jean's flowered aprons while she used a spatula to push bacon around a cast-iron pan. A tray of freshly baked muffins sat cooling on the counter beside her.

"Good morning, Nova! I thought I'd throw something together. It won't be as good as Aunt Jean's breakfasts, but it's better than cold cereal." Connie smiled. "It's great to see you again."

"It's good to see you too, Connie." Nova managed a smile, even as she felt the loss of her aunt all over again.

Maybe she could find a way to bring Aunt Jean back too. The enormity of the task at hand hit her again, and she felt like going back upstairs and climbing into bed.

"Are you all right? You look like you've seen a ghost.

Although I wouldn't be surprised in this house!" Connie laughed.

"I had a... dream. It seemed so real."

"Well, you're in the Garden Room. You'll probably have lots of dreams in there. Aunt Jean always said that room was magical." She smiled. "Aunt Jean gave all the guest rooms names."

"Really? She never said anything about that before, uh…" Nova wasn't sure how to wrap up that thought or even if her statement would make sense. She had no memory of what had happened previously at Willow Hill in this timeline.

"Oh, yes. The Western-themed room is the 'Old Fart Room'!"

"Seriously? Why?" Nova laughed.

"Well, it was before I was ever here, but according to Aunt Jean, Bill never really got into the whole steeplechase thing with the horses. If he'd had his way, we would have been a Western barn, complete with calf roping and barrel racing. He even bought himself a quarter horse named Cisco and a Western saddle. He rode all over the place, wearing a cowboy hat and boots. When I started coming out here to see Justin, Bill let me take Cisco out a few times, just to see what it was like to ride a 'real horse'! Don't tell Justin, but I liked riding in a Western saddle much more than riding English.

And Cisco was as gentle as a lamb, but he could run like you wouldn't believe. Quarter horses are very fast for short distances, which is why they make great barrel racers. They have powerful back ends and can turn on a dime! Of course, as far as Justin is concerned, there's nothing like racing and jumping fences." Connie put the plate of bacon and the muffins on the table with two glasses of orange juice and motioned for Nova to sit down. "Dig in before it gets cold."

Nova sat down and took a muffin and two pieces of bacon. "This is delicious. Aunt Jean would be proud."

Connie seemed pleased by the compliment. "Thanks."

"What happened to Cisco?" Nova asked between bites.

"When Uncle Bill died, Aunt Jean retired that sweet horse and let him live out his days on the farm. She said it was sad because he'd wait at the gate for Bill every day. Bill always took him a treat first thing in the morning—an apple or carrots, sometimes a cube of sugar. It broke Aunt Jean's heart that he kept looking for Bill, so she started going out there with something for him. She did that every morning until he passed away too, just a year or so after Bill. She buried Cisco about twenty feet from Bill in the family graveyard at the back of the property. Of course, the county doesn't know that there's a horse buried on the family plot!" She laughed. "Have you ever been back there?"

"No." Nova shuddered. She had forgotten about there being a graveyard at Willow Hill. "How many people and… uh… horses are buried there?"

"Oh, there's only Bill, Georgia, Patrick, Justin's parents, and Cisco back there right now," Connie said as if burying loved ones in your backyard with their horses was the most natural thing in the world.

"Who's Patrick?" Nova asked, hoping it wasn't a dog or some other pet but unable to quell her morbid curiosity. She also wondered why Justin's parents were buried there, but hesitated to ask.

"Patrick was the old caretaker of the property. He owned this land before Jean and Bill bought it, but it was too much for him. Your aunt and uncle let him stay on the property in his little house, and he sort of watched over things. They offered to build him a new place, but he didn't want it. I'm not sure he actually did any real work, but he was a sweet old guy."

"That was nice of Aunt Jean and Uncle Bill," Nova said sincerely.

"They were special people." Connie smiled.

"So tell me why Georgia called the Western guestroom the 'Old Fart Room.'"

"Well, like I said, Georgia was determined to have an English barn. Every so often, Bill and Georgia would have a *discussion* about it and he'd end up in the guest room for a night or two. Aunt Jean decorated it Western in his honor, but Georgia named it!”

“That’s hysterical!”

“We have three other guest rooms, all named. Your dad’s in the Presidential Room because your aunt always said that if the president came to visit, that’s where she’d put him. Then there are two more guest rooms on the other side of the house. The farthest one down the hall is the Sandman Room, and the other is the Captain’s Quarters. Those are the rooms that Michael and his family always take when they come. It made sense when the kids were all little because that’s the quietest part of the house. Aunt Jean used to tell them the story of the sandman every night before they went to sleep. There are four bunk beds in the Sandman Room, so she’d turn off all the lights, sit on the floor, and tell them the story. They were usually all asleep before she got to the end. Of course, the Captain’s Quarters is where Michael and Julia slept.”

“How old are Michael’s kids now?”

“Oh let’s see… Miles is thirteen, I think. He’s the oldest. That means Henry is eleven, and the twins are nine.”

“Twins?” Nova perked up. “Must run in the family.”

“I guess so. They’re girls too—Maisy and Lily.”

“I bet they love the horses.” Nova thought about Marshall. He would have loved having other kids to hang out with at the barn. Before she could stop them, tears welled up in her eyes and spilled over. Embarrassed, Nova wiped them away with the hem of her shirt.

“I understand, Nova. I miss Aunt Jean too.” Connie came over and put her arms around Nova.

“I was just thinking…” Nova wished she could tell Connie that it wasn’t just Aunt Jean who was gone.

Connie kept talking while she loaded dishes into the dishwasher. “You need a distraction. How about helping me with James when we’re through with breakfast? Justin is down at the barn, showing him the horses, but that only keeps the little guy happy for so long! He’s only a few weeks old, so I don’t know how much he takes in, but Justin loves carrying him around showing him things."

"He's a lucky little boy. I bet he'll be following Justin around the barn before you know it." She thought again of Marshall. Justin had been so patient with her little brother. He was going to make a great dad.

"You're right. Justin can't wait to have his little sidekick tagging along. He talks about it all the time! Anyway, I need to go get the baby so Justin can do some repairs to the paddock gate. Want to come with me?"

"I'd love to, but my dad and I are leaving today."

"You are? Why so soon?" Connie was clearly disappointed.

"Something with Dad's publisher. We just have to go through some things with Michael this morning, then head back home." At least that part was true.

"Well, you have to promise to come back soon. Looks like Justin and I will be here. And James of course." She smiled. "I can't get over the fact that your aunt left us so much. The barn, the horses... so much land. Seventy-five acres! And little James won't ever have to worry about college because it's all paid for. It's overwhelming. Of course, she always treated Justin like a son. He never really understood why. I mean, he appreciated it of course, but he always wondered why they were so kind to him. I mean, Justin's dad did work for Uncle Bill, but it was more than that. They were like real family."

"I noticed that... uh... before." Nova looked at Connie, but she didn't seem the least bit confused by her statement. Maybe they'd been here often over the years in this reality.

"Well, I'm glad she left your dad the house. Michael doesn't need it, and Jean always had a soft spot for Dayton."

"I'm kind of surprised she didn't leave it to you and Justin since you live here and all."

"Heavens no! It's too big for us, and we'd already cleared a spot for ours on the other side of the property. Justin drew the plans himself," she said proudly. "We just had an architect make a few adjustments. I can't believe we have the money to do it now. I think it'll be perfect for our family, even if we have a couple more kids." Connie blushed a little. "Justin said he'd like to have a houseful. I told him I'd agree to one more, maybe two. After that, he has to be the one to have them!"

"I think that if the guys had to have the babies, the human race would die out."

Connie threw her head back and laughed. "You said it, sister! I'm not even sure *I* want to do it again. James was worth it though. He's the cutest thing I ever saw. You'll have to come back and bring your mom and Alana. I bet they'd love to see him."

"I will," Nova said, not sure if that was true or not. Without Aunt Jean and Marshall, Willow Hill wasn't the same. "Connie… can I ask you something?"

"Of course." Connie smiled.

"How did Aunt Jean die? I mean, no one really said what happened. If you don't want to talk about it, I understand. I just… I don't know. I want to know."

Connie appeared to be gathering her thoughts. Then she shook her head. "It was the strangest thing, in a way. We were all on the porch—Justin, the baby, Aunt Jean, and me—talking about something. I don't remember what. Aunt Jean said she had to go upstairs for a few minutes. None of us thought a thing about it. She said she'd be right back down, so we waited for her. It was a beautiful night. There wasn't a cloud in the sky. I remember Justin saying that we should bring the telescope down from the attic and look at stars. There's almost no light pollution out here at night, and you can see everything. I don't know much about the constellations, but Justin is something of an expert on the subject. He took several astronomy courses in college."

Connie smiled wistfully. "He brought that down a few days ago." She pointed at the corner of the kitchen, beside the fireplace, where a telescope stood. "We've been taking it out on clear nights. Next time you're down here, we'll have to look at stars."

"I'd love that. But what about…"

"Sorry, I got sidetracked. That's just me, I'm afraid. Justin laughs and calls it chasing butterflies. 'Oh, Connie's chasing butterflies again!' he says." Connie grinned. "I don't mind. Aunt Jean always told me to ignore it because she had some things she could tell me about Justin too! She said Justin daydreamed so much in school that he once sat there staring out the window after everyone else had left the classroom and the teacher came over and startled him by dropping a book on his desk."

"I can relate to that!" Nova said. "I get my mind on something and have no idea what's going on around me."

"Well, there you go. I guess we all do it." She smiled. "Anyway, like I was saying, Aunt Jean went into the house. After a while, James got restless and we realized it had been over thirty minutes. Since it was getting late, Justin went in to tell her we were calling it a night. The horses start making a racket pretty early and we didn't want to be up too late. I waited for Justin to come back out so we could walk down to the barn together, but he was inside so long I finally took James back to the apartment by myself. Justin came in about twenty minutes later and told me. She was lying on her bed, still dressed and wearing the apron she'd cooked in. He said she looked so peaceful he thought she was sleeping. We don't really know what happened. The coroner said it was probably her heart, but he couldn't be sure. She left strict instructions that there was to be no autopsy when she died."

"That must have been so hard on both of you, finding her like that." Nova tried to wrap her brain around the whole scenario. Aunt Jean had helped Nova travel just before she died in a different timeline. It didn't make sense.

"It was real hard. Justin's parents are dead, and mine are overseas because of my dad's job. Aunt Jean was the only family we had here," Connie said tearfully.

"You have us too." Nova assured her.

"Thank you, Nova. That means a lot." Connie wiped

her eyes. "I wish you didn't have to go."

"We'll be back soon. I promise."

"I'll hold you to that." Connie smiled.

"I guess I'd better get my things together so I'll be ready to leave. Can I help you before I go?"

"No, I'm almost finished in here. Just be sure to come say goodbye before you leave."

"I will."

Nova took off upstairs to her room, grateful to have a little time alone to collect her thoughts. An image of Aunt Jean lying on the bed in her room kept popping into her head. She couldn't imagine finding her aunt that way. It still didn't make sense why she would have passed away so suddenly. She'd never been sick and seemed so full of life. Nova couldn't shake the nagging feeling that she was to blame. But how was that even possible? Aunt Jean had died in a different timeline.

Nova paused at the guest room door and stared down the hallway toward Aunt Jean's room, wrestling with the urge to go see it for herself. Maybe her aunt had left a clue, like she had with the journal. Maybe there would be something left behind that only Nova would notice.

Nova pulled her door closed and made her way down the hall to her aunt's room. When she reached for the knob, she half expected it to be locked. But it turned easily. She stepped inside, closed the door, and flicked on the light.

She'd never been in her aunt's room before, but it was as she had imagined it would be. Everything about it was comfortable and unpretentious, just like Aunt Jean. An oversized armchair sat next to a large window overlooking the garden and pasture. She could picture her aunt sitting there after a long day, enjoying the beautiful landscape. The bed was a four-poster, similar to the one in Nova's room, but heavier and less ornate. The patchwork quilt that covered the mattress looked homemade. Nova climbed onto the bed and laid her head on the pillows, closing her eyes and breathing in the scent of lavender.

"I miss you so much," she whispered.

The temptation to travel again to see her aunt was overwhelming, but Aunt Jean had told her not to unless it was absolutely necessary. Nova's head started to hurt a little, so she decided to let it go for now. Later, she would read more of the journal. Somewhere in Evelyn's revelations, she'd find the answer. Nova was determined to have all of her family together at once, no matter how many times she had to switch.

She heard Dayton and Michael down the hall, outside her room, so she jumped off the bed and stuck her head out of the door.

"Nova! There you are. What are you doing?"

"I just wanted to see Aunt Jean's room."

Michael stuck his hands in his pockets, clearly uncomfortable. "No one's been in there since she died. I know we need to go through her things, but—"

"I'd like to leave it like it is if that's okay," Nova interrupted.

"Fine with me. It's your house." Michael looked relieved. "If you see anything you want though, go ahead and take it."

"I don't know. It'd feel funny taking Aunt Jean's things," Nova admitted, thinking about the coin.

"Okay, honey," Dayton spoke up. "We'll be downstairs."

Nova pulled the door closed behind her and walked slowly to her room. She quickly changed into clean shorts, a white cotton blouse, and sandals before packing and heading downstairs to find Michael and her dad.

CHAPTER 15

Nova found them at the dining room table, going over the details of the will. While they poured over the paper work, Nova went through the motions of looking around the house for any items that she might want to take home.

By one o'clock, she was back in the attic, looking through the shelves and boxes. It would have taken months to catalog that place. She finally decided to keep the coin from the trunk and her great-grandmother's journal, but leave everything else just as it was. It seemed wrong to remove any of Aunt Jean's things. They belonged at Willow Hill. As soon as she was back in her room, she picked the coin up off of the night table and dropped it into her pocket. She could hear Dayton and Michael talking at the bottom of the stairs.

"I really wish we could stay, but it's just not possible. There's an issue with my publisher that needs my attention. I'm afraid it can't be handled from here."

Nova couldn't help but smile. *I guess I know where I get my ability to lie convincingly. He's not making any sense and Michael is still buying it.*

"I hope you at least come back soon. This is your house now."

Michael's words hit home for Nova. *This is* our *house.* It still hadn't fully sunk in.

"I'm so glad you aren't planning to sell it, Dayton. I know that would please Aunt Jean. This place meant the world to her."

"I can't imagine selling," Dayton answered sincerely.

"Well, all right then." Michael looked up as Nova appeared at the top of the stars. "Did you find anything you wanted?"

"Not really. I mean... I just think it should all stay here." *All except for Evelyn's journal about time travel and the pirate coin from the attic.* She smiled as she reached into her pocket and felt the cool gold medallion. For some reason, it made her feel connected to the house.

"Sounds good." Michael seemed pleased. "And next time you're back here, that attic door will close all the way. I've already planned to fix it before I leave. Your dad says he's not all that handy around the house." Michael grinned at Nova.

Dayton laughed. "That's right, you two. Yuk it up."

"That's okay, Dad. I love you even if you can't nail two boards together," Nova said sweetly.

Michael looked at his watch, then back at Dayton. "Hey, it's almost three o'clock. If you're ready, we need to leave for the airport."

"Yes, we do!" Dayton seemed slightly alarmed that they'd let it get so late. "Our flight leaves at four forty-five. Get your things, Nova. Mine are already down here."

Nova dashed back to her room and grabbed her bag, then she took one last look around before pulling the door closed. As she walked down the hall, she pictured Aunt Jean at the bottom of the stairs, waiting for her. It would have been just like her to find a way to come back to the moment that would achieve the most shock value. "Close your mouth, honey. You'll catch a fly!" she'd say. Nova smiled just thinking about her aunt pulling a stunt like that. After all, Aunt Jean had known last summer that she'd be dead by the next year because Nova had traveled back and told her. She'd had plenty of time to work something out.

When Nova stepped out of the hallway and onto the landing, the only person she saw was her dad. He was waiting at the front door.

"Come on, Nova." He sounded impatient.

"Okay." Nova glanced back down the hall toward the Garden Room, wondering when she'd be back at Willow Hill. As she descended the stairs, she heard the clock somewhere in the house, chiming the hour. A chill ran up her spine. *I'll see you again, Aunt Jean. I promise.*

They piled into Michael's rental car and headed off. Almost an hour later, he dropped them off at the Charlotte airport. After hasty goodbyes, they dashed through security and arrived out of breath at their gate just as an attendant was making the announcement that boarding was delayed forty-five minutes.

Nova didn't feel like talking, so she used the time to browse the gift shop next to the waiting area. She went through the motions of examining the items lining the shelves, but spent most of the time planning how she would tell her dad about her visit with Aunt Jean. Now that she'd had time to think about it, the weight of her disappointment was crushing. Her aunt hadn't given her any guidance, except to look for the journal in the old chest. Nova had read it cover to cover, and so far had more questions than answers. Going back in time to actually talk to Evelyn was out of the question since she had died before Nova was born. Marshall seemed to be slipping further and further away. Her only hope was deciphering the more cryptic entries in Evelyn's journal.

Nova noticed the clerk behind the register eye her suspiciously, watching her every move with a pinched expression. He obviously thought she was up to something because she had circled the displays three or four times without buying anything. Several other batches of travelers had come and gone, making their purchases quickly and darting off to catch their flights. She'd probably been in the tiny store at least twenty minutes. No wonder he was suspicious.

Deciding to wrap up her tour of the shop, Nova paid for a pack of gum and joined her dad in the waiting area just as the announcement to board came over the speakers. They made their way onto the plane and found their seats halfway down. As soon as Nova sat down, a little boy behind her, who appeared to be about five years old, started kicking her seat. She turned and gave him a sweet smile.

"Hi!" he said loudly.

"Hi. What's your name?" Maybe if she distracted him, he'd forget about kicking the seat.

"Charlie!" He apparently only had one volume.

"Charlie, not so loud." His mother smiled apologetically.

Nova smiled back before facing forward again. It was going to be a long flight.

"Just remember, you were that age once," her dad whispered.

"Yeah. That helps." She tried not to sound too sarcastic.

"So let's think about something else. Did you read any more of Evelyn's journal?" he asked.

Nova took a deep breath. "Yes, but… something happened at Aunt Jean's."

"What happened?" he asked, immediately on edge.

"I talked to her."

"Who?"

"Aunt Jean."

Dayton stared at her, his expression impossible to read. Charlie kicked her seat again.

His mother leaned forward. "I'm sorry. If it helps, he'll been asleep before the seat belt signs go off."

Nova turned around and smiled. "It's okay."

The woman gave her a grateful look. When she faced forward again, Nova glanced at Dayton. His face was the same—unreadable.

"Dad. Say something," she whispered.

"You traveled?" He sounded angry.

"I… *visited.*"

"What do you mean? Do you realize that other things

could be different now? We may go home to all kinds of other problems!" His voice was starting to carry.

Nova held her finger to her lips. "Maybe we should talk about this in the car later."

Dayton leaned toward her and lowered his voice. "I need to know what you did. I don't want any more surprises."

"Nothing will be different. Don't you remember Aunt Jean telling us about visiting? I only stayed for a few minutes, until I could feel the connection getting weaker. Then I jumped right back to where I started. Nothing changed. As long as you go right back, nothing changes. You end up where you started. That's how it was with me. I swear it'll be okay."

Nova waited for him to say something else, but he seemed to be processing it. He closed his eyes and leaned his head back against the seat. Apparently, they were giving it a rest for now, so Nova did the same.

They were in the air, halfway to Boston, when Dayton nudged her. "So how was it? Seeing Aunt Jean?"

Nova gave herself a moment to wake up and collect her thoughts. She'd known exactly what she was going to say before, but now her brain didn't want to cooperate.

"Give me a second. I was asleep." Nova rubbed her eyes and tried to focus, picturing the moment she had stepped into the kitchen and seen her aunt alive and well. "It was amazing. Wonderful... and a little weird. Does that make sense?"

"Well, sure. She was supposed to be dead."

"Right." She chuckled. "She was just the same though. She was in the kitchen baking muffins. It was just like before, like nothing had happened." Nova's eyes filled with tears. "It was amazing. She didn't realize at first that I'd

traveled back to see her because we were all there—you,

Mom, Alana, and me." Nova wiped her eyes on her shirt absently.

"You saw us?" Dayton was incredulous.

"No. You were upstairs sleeping. It was last summer, right after my birthday."

"So… if you were already there—"

"Was another me upstairs too?" Nova interrupted.

"Yeah."

"No, thank God. She said there's only one of each of us, so that can't happen. And she guessed right away that she must be dead in the time I came from. Her reaction was surprising, like she found it amusing. It didn't seem to bother her."

"Incredible." Dayton shook his head. "What did she say about Marshall?"

"Well, she remembered him. But there wasn't anything she could do because we were still in the same timeline. She remembered an image of him, but not in this life."

"Did she tell you how to get him back?" he asked, disappointed.

"She said I have to work the problem from here. She also told me about her mother's journal. That's why she left me the chest. So I'd have it."

"That's it? We just have to figure it out for ourselves?" he asked.

"I guess so."

Dayton seemed to be processing everything. "So what's the plan?"

"We need to figure out what Evelyn meant about using someone else's timeline and the other possibilities she hinted at. She mentioned something called a tapestry toward the end of her journal. She talked about timelines weaving together. I couldn't make sense of it. That's why we need to talk to Grandma Kate again. Even if she doesn't know how to do any of the things that Evelyn was talking about, something may click when she reads her journal. Grandma Kate's the only one left who actually lived with Evelyn, so she's still our best shot. She may remember something that

Aunt Jean forgot. Something Evelyn said that explains what it all means."

Dayton frowned. "I dread the thought of going back there."

"I know. Me too, but we don't have a choice."

"We need to go home first."

"Why?" Nova was ready to head straight back to her grandmother's house.

"I just need a day, okay? This has all happened so fast. I want to see Alana. You know, just in case something happens at Mother's and we don't see her for a while."

His statement hit her like a brick wall. "Okay, Dad. We'll go home first."

"Do you think you can come up with any theories from what my grandmother wrote?" Dayton asked hopefully.

"I haven't yet. But I promise I will." Nova hoped she could keep her word. Coming up with a plan using Evelyn's journal would be difficult since all she did was hint at possibilities and describe things that made no sense. Nova needed another brain in on this with her. She decided there was no time like the present. "Dad, there's something else."

"What?" He sounded nervous. "You didn't do something else, did you?"

"No, nothing like that. When we get home, I think we need to tell Alana everything. She's probably a traveler too since we're twins."

"Fraternal twins, honey. So there are no guarantees. If she isn't a traveler, all hell could break loose." Dayton frowned.

Nova couldn't be deterred. "I think we need to risk it. One thing Aunt Jean said and Evelyn wrote about was that fellow travelers can lend power to each other. Aunt Jean did it for me. I'm sure of it."

"I wonder why Aunt Jean didn't say anything about that in the garden."

"I think she was probably trying not to overload us with information right away. She told me in the kitchen when

I visited. If Alana is a traveler too, she could help us. Even if she doesn't know how to travel yet. She'd still have power to lend me if I was doing it. I don't think I could have brought Alana back without Aunt Jean's help. Maybe doing something big takes more power than one person has."

"I'm still not sure about telling your sister. If she's a traveler too, why doesn't she know about any other timelines? We've changed a couple of times you know."

"Yes, but she wasn't around in the others."

He nodded. "Yeah, you're right. I wasn't thinking about that."

"We have to tell her. She has a right to know about her family."

"What if she's not a traveler? What if we tell her and it blows up in our faces?"

"Then we've screwed up. Who cares? We're not staying here."

Dayton thought for a moment before responding. When he did, he sounded tired. "Fine. When we get home we'll tell her."

"Thanks, Dad." Nova squeezed his arm just as Charlie resumed kicking her seat.

By the time they landed in Boston, she had decided she was never having children.

Dayton grabbed a couple of sandwiches in the deli beside their gate and Nova dutifully choked hers down in the shuttle on the way to their car, even though she wasn't the least bit hungry. She pretended to sleep for the first hour of their drive home from the airport. The truth was she was anything but sleepy. Her mind was in overdrive, thinking about the journal and what it all meant. She couldn't wait to talk to her sister, to convince her that she belonged to a family of time travelers. She figured the best plan was to just be straight with her. *Alana, we're time travelers. You can probably do it too. Want to go to Burger Barn for lunch?*

Nova stifled a giggle, and Dayton shot her a concerned look.

"I'm okay, Dad."

"Since you're awake now, do you want to talk?"

"I'm really tired. Can we talk later?"

"Maybe you're tired because you're sleeping too much." He sounded frustrated. Nova couldn't blame him, but if she told him she wanted to tell Alana on her own, he wouldn't understand. Since she didn't respond instantly, Dayton said, "I think we need to talk. We need to plan how we're telling Alana."

"I know. Can't we wait until we get home?"

"We won't have any privacy at home."

"I'm coming up with some theories. Maybe it would be better to tell her when I have them worked out in my head. I don't want to break my train of thought." That worked.

"Okay, firefly. You keep thinking. I know you'll come up with something." Dayton smiled hopefully.

Nova felt awful deceiving him. She'd have to make good on the whole "coming up with a theory" promise. *Alana, I hope you're brilliant. I need help.* Nova leaned her head back against the seat and closed her eyes again, going over and over what she planned to say to her sister.

When they pulled into the driveway, the porch light was on but the rest of the house was dark. It wasn't unusual for Celeste to go to bed early since she ran every morning around six thirty. Alana's room was on the back of the house, so there was no way to know if she was up or not. Nova hoped her sister was already in bed. She was exhausted from the emotional strain of the last few days and didn't really feel like talking to Alana tonight.

Dayton unlocked the front door, and they stepped inside to a quiet house. When Nova tiptoed down the hallway to her room, she noticed that there was no light coming from under Alana's bedroom door. Relieved, she set her bag in her room, showered quickly, and changed for bed.

Dayton tapped on her door a few minutes later. "Talk tomorrow?"

"Sure, Dad," Nova answered, crawling into bed and

pulling up the sheet.

She heard him walking back up the hallway to his room. The bed felt heavenly, and Nova let herself drift off. She'd figure things out tomorrow.

CHAPTER 16

Shortly after nine in the morning, Alana stuck her head in the door. "Hey, little sister! How was the trip down south?"

Nova sat up, rubbing her eyes. "It was okay. Kind of weird without Aunt Jean there."

"Yeah, I'm sure," Alana said brightly. "Want to hear what went on while you were gone?"

"Let me wake up first, okay?" Nova swung her legs over the side of the bed and stood up. "Hang on."

She went up the hall to the bathroom and splashed some water on her face before coming back to her room and climbing onto her bed again.

"Okay. I'm all ears," Nova said.

"Well, Ethan came by the day after you and Dad left just to see if I'd heard from you. He's so in love! It's a little nauseating. Anyway, Mom told him she'd have you call next time we heard from you, which we never did of course."

"Dad didn't call Mom at all while we were gone?"

"Of course he did. But you didn't call, so I guess that kind of let us off the hook with Ethan. What's the deal with him? I've never known you to get so *friendly* with a guy this quick before." Alana sat down beside Nova on the bed.

"What's the story, little sister?"

Nova avoided the question. "I'm sorry I didn't call you. Things were pretty busy at Aunt Jean's. I just forgot."

"You're not gonna tell me what gives with Ethan?"

Alana persisted.

"Maybe later." Her relationship with Ethan would make more sense to Alana after she knew about the family gift.

"Whatever." Alana was clearly disappointed. Neither of them said anything for a minute. Alana finally broke the silence. "I kind of wish I'd gone with you to Willow Hill. I've been thinking about it a lot since you were gone. Do you remember how Aunt Jean used to take us out on trail rides when we were little?"

"Sure," Nova lied. As far as she knew, she'd never been on a trail ride in her life.

"You were so scared. I told you there was a word I could say that would make your horse buck you off and run back to the barn and you believed me! I got in so much trouble for that. Dad wouldn't let me ride the whole rest of the time we were there that summer. How old were we? Eight?"

"I don't remember," Nova said honestly. "I'm sorry I was such a coward though."

"You were okay. I was just being mean. I'm sorry." Alana hugged her. "I'm sorry too about the whole Paris thing. You know, getting mad because you wouldn't decide right there at the party. I know you like to think about things. Not like me. I always jump in and think later, don't I?"

Nova smiled. "Yeah, you kind of do. But that's one of the things I love about you."

"I know we're going to London first and then taking the train to Paris. But you pick where you want to go after that. Deal?"

"Deal."

"I need to call David. We're supposed to do something today." Alana got up and walked toward the door.

It's now or never. "Alana, I need to talk to you about something."

"Okay, shoot." Alana plopped down on the bed again and waited.

"Promise me you'll think about what I'm saying. Don't freak out or anything, okay?"

"Jeez, what is it? Just so you know, telling someone not to freak out is a great way to make them actually freak out. You're not pregnant or dying or anything, are you?"

"Good Lord, no!" Nova laughed nervously. "I just have some… information to share with you. It's pretty amazing information. You might have a hard time believing it, that's all."

Alana cocked her head to the side. "Do you believe it?"

"Of course. I *know* it," Nova responded earnestly.

"Then I'll believe it too. So go ahead. Spill." Alana grinned.

"Okay. You know that we have two sides to our family—the Grants and the Richardsons."

"Duh." Alana was already impatient.

"Well, the Grant side has something special about it. They—or *we*—have a gift. An ability."

"And what is this ability?" Alana asked, amused. "Obviously it's not math because I suck at it."

Nova hesitated then plunged in. "It's time travel."

"Time travel," Alana repeated, staring at Nova as if she'd sprouted feathers.

"Right. Well, some of them…some of *us* can. Most, I think. We've been doing it for as long as anyone can remember." Nova waited for a reaction, but Alana just continued to stare at her. "What do you think about that?"

"I think you're medicated, and not in a good way. That's what I think. So what's the real thing you wanted to tell me?" Alana asked.

"That's it. We can travel in time. As a matter of fact, I've done it myself."

"You have? How fascinating. Oh please, tell me about it." Alana leaned forward, feigning interest.

"You don't have to be sarcastic. I'm serious."

"You're nuts. I'm gonna get some breakfast. Want to

come?" Alana clearly intended to be through with this conversation.

"You don't want to know anything about it? I tell you we can travel in time and you're not curious at all?" Nova was incredulous. Obviously, Alana thought she was joking.

"You're real funny. Let's get something to eat before I starve."

"Wait! I can prove it!" Nova had an idea. "Give me fifteen minutes."

"Why?"

"Just do it. I have to show you something."

Alana sighed. "Okay, you have fifteen minutes." She was getting annoyed.

"Look at the time. It's nine thirty, right?"

"Nine twenty-eight," Alana corrected.

"Okay, nine-twenty-eight." Nova grabbed Alana's hand and pulled her up the hall and into the den.

"What are we doing?" Alana demanded. "You're making me nervous."

"We need to sit here for… I don't know… like, ten minutes or so."

"Why? What's happening in ten minutes?" Alana asked anxiously. "Besides, you said fifteen."

"That's for the whole experiment. This is the waiting part. Just trust me. What can we do for ten minutes?" Nova glanced around the room and zeroed in on a stack of puzzles by the entertainment center. "We'll do a puzzle!"

"Seriously, are you high?"

Nova burst out laughing. "Oh my God, you sound like Ethan!"

"Ethan asked you if you were high? I'm sensing a theme here."

"Just wait." Nova dumped out the puzzle and started looking for the edge pieces. "Are you helping me or what?"

Alana reluctantly sorted through the puzzle pieces with her, grumbling about having better things to do besides babysitting her demented sister while they waited for the men in white coats to show up.

After ten minutes, Nova stood and announced it was time.

"Time for what?" Alana stood up too.

"Just wait here for a few more minutes. I swear it won't be longer than that. Promise me you'll wait until I get back."

"Okay. I promise." Alana sat down again, frowning.

Nova ran to her room and closed the door. She lay back on her bed and tried to relax, taking long, slow breaths. After a few minutes, nothing had happened. Alana was probably getting even more impatient. Nova squeezed her eyes shut and focused, picturing them sitting on the bed just before she'd dragged her sister into the den. She kept her body still and her breathing slow and rhythmic. Alana was telling her the time—nine twenty-eight.

Nova's brain struggled to find some sound to latch on to. Somewhere outside, a lawnmower was running. That would have to do. She honed in on the sound of the machine, finally feeling her mind lock in. She saw Alana looking at her watch—nine twenty-eight. Nova felt the familiar floating sensation, then an almost imperceptible drop, like a slight dip in the road.

She opened her eyes and there was Alana, sitting across from her with a shocked expression.

"What the—!" Alana gasped. "How did we get back here?"

"Time travel!" Nova grinned. "See?"

"Holy crap! That was the weirdest thing ever! What did you do to me?"

"Nothing. I just went back to 9:28. It's not that hard to jump back a few minutes." Nova smiled. "And you know what the best part is?"

"What's the best part?" Alana asked, hanging on Nova's every word.

"You can do it too!" Nova announced excitedly.

"Wait… what? I can do what?"

"If you weren't a traveler too, you wouldn't have noticed the time switch! But you did! That means you can do it too!"

"I need to sit down. Oh crap. I am sitting. Nova, this is messed up." Alana shivered a little. "Okay. You have my full attention. Tell me what's going on."

"First, you know I told you that *some* of the Grant family are able to time travel?"

"Yeah, I think I got that."

"Well, you're one of them—a time traveler. If you weren't, you wouldn't have noticed you were repeating time. But you did notice."

"Why did we have to do the whole thing in the den first?"

"I didn't want to have to tell you everything again. I just figured I'd go back to the point where you needed proof. Do you understand?"

Alana shook her head. "No. But go on."

"Okay. There's so much I want to share with you, but I need to tell you something kind of awful first."

"What is it?"

"In some of the timelines… you weren't here."

"What do you mean I wasn't here?" Alana asked, alarmed.

"You know you had a heart condition when you were born."

"Of course."

"Well, in our first timeline, you only lived five years."

"What happened to me?" Alana's voice was barely audible.

"We were swimming. I guess the strain on your heart was too much and you went under. They couldn't revive you."

Alana's face was white as a sheet. "I've had that dream… lots of times. I just thought it was a nightmare."

"No. It's a memory from a previous timeline. It

happened. I don't really remember the details, but I remember us in the pool. Mom and Dad didn't know about your heart condition. After you died, Dad tried to go back and save you. He thought he could have you checked out when you were born, have tests done that would show the problem. But something happened that time during delivery and you died right after you were born."

Alana shook her head. "Wow. Sucks to be me, I guess." She managed a half smile. "So how come I'm here now? Dad must have gone back again."

"Not exactly." Nova hesitated, not sure how to explain that he'd never tried again.

"What do you mean? Obviously I'm here, so he must have done something."

"He didn't." Nova studied her sister's face. "I did."

"How did you go back in time and tell the doctors I had a heart condition? Didn't they wonder who the strange sixteen-year-old girl was?"

"Alana… this is where it gets complicated."

Alana frowned. "It's already complicated. Just tell me."

"Okay. In the first timeline that *I* actually remember, you died at birth. I didn't even know I had a twin sister. Mom and Dad decided not to tell me and—" Nova nearly included Marshall before catching herself. She wasn't sure how to tell Alana about her little brother. "They never told me about you."

"So let me get this straight. I died at birth and Dad just moved on?"

"No! It's not like that. He was devastated."

"But not devastated enough to bother changing it?"

"It's not that simple! He'd already tried once and lost the five years he'd had with you. He was scared to try again."

"This family *gift* doesn't sound like such a great thing," Alana said bitterly. "Nice to know that my parents were able to go on like I never existed."

"This isn't going at all like I planned. I'm doing a

terrible job of explaining things."

Alana huffed. "You're doing fine. Go on."

"Dad was devastated when he lost you. He asked Grandma Kate to help him get you back, but she refused."

Alana stood and started for the door.

Nova jumped up. "Wait! Where are you going?"

"I'm gonna talk to my parents!" Alana replied angrily.

"Stop! You don't understand!" Nova grabbed her arm. "Please let me finish!"

"What else is there to say?"

"There's a lot to say! Just wait! Dad died in that timeline too."

Alana wheeled around. "He did? How?" She sat on the bed again, her anger obviously gone.

"It was a car accident on the bridge the first day of school. He went through the railing into the river. They never found his body."

"Oh my God…" Alana whispered.

"It was awful. We all sort of died a little with him. Mom was the worst. She was so depressed and didn't care about anything anymore. She worried about money and kept dying her hair and running for hours. You can't imagine how awful it was. We were miserable. I didn't care about anything." *Except Marshall.* "Then about nine months after the accident, at the end of the school year, I got up one morning and everything was different. Mom was her old self.

She was cooking breakfast and seemed… happy. Her hair was back to its normal color." Once again, she avoided mentioning Marshall. "It was weird. Then on the bus, I tried to sit with my best friend, Delilah, but she acted like she barely knew me."

"Are you talking about Delilah Davenport? She was your best friend?"

"Yeah," Nova answered.

"You must have been desperate."

"She wasn't that bad. Besides, she was the only one

who stuck around after the accident. It was my fault, really. I guess I changed a lot. Delilah was the only one who didn't seem to mind the new me." Nova shook her head, remembering how lonely that year would have been without Dee. She'd have to make a point to be friendlier to her when classes started back in the fall.

"Okay, so Delilah was your best friend, but she didn't act like she knew you. Then what?" Alana was clearly impatient for her to get on with the story.

"When I got to school, things were even more bizarre," Nova continued. "My first class wasn't my class anymore, and I had a boyfriend following me around and asking if I was on drugs!" Nova chuckled. "Seriously, you would have loved it. I thought I was crazy."

Alana's mouth was hanging open. *Must be a family trait.*

"Where was I?" Alana asked.

"Still dead."

"Oh. Right."

"Don't worry. I'm getting to the part where you're not dead anymore."

"What a relief." Alana tried to sound light, but Nova could tell she was on edge. "Okay, school was nuts, so I bolted for home with Ethan. It was strange, but in a way, it felt natural to have him with me."

Alana smiled. "He was the boyfriend, I'm guessing."

"Yes. We walked home from school. When we got here, Dad's Mustang was in the driveway."

When Nova paused to let that sink in, Alana arched an eyebrow. "So?"

"He was supposed to be dead! His car was supposed to be mangled in a junkyard somewhere. But it was sitting there good as new!"

"Oh, right. I forgot. What happened when you saw it?" Nova had to give Alana credit. She was adjusting to this new reality remarkably well. "Come on, little sister! Tell me."

"Okay. So I saw Dad's car in the driveway and I passed out and hit my head on the concrete. When I came to, Dad was there. I tried to talk to him, but paramedics came and took me to the hospital. That's when I realized that no one else thought anything was weird. Just me. To everyone else, it was like he'd never left. It was like something out of one of his books. A couple of days after I got home from the hospital, I started looking around his office, trying to figure out what happened. That's when I found your birth certificate." Nova decided not to mention that the death certificate was in her file too.

"What did Mom and Dad say about that?"

"Nothing. I didn't ask them. I did eventually confront Dad, but I never talked to Mom about it. She doesn't know about the Grant family *gift*."

"Seriously? How could she not know?"

"Dad never told her. And there weren't any other family members around to let it slip. Grandma Kate moved him away from the rest of the Grants when Dad was little because she never wanted him to time travel. Something bad happened to her when she was young, and she swore she'd never travel again and neither would Dad. He was completely out of touch with the rest of the family. That's why he screwed it up so badly when he tried go back and save you.

No one told him how to do it. He just managed to travel when he was upset. He didn't have any real control. After the first time, when going back made you die at birth, he gave up, I guess. He believed Grandma Kate was right that traveling just causes more tragedy."

"So why am I here now?"

"When I finally confronted Dad, I found out that when his car went into the river that day, he traveled. It wasn't something he tried to do. It just happened. He was thinking about me as his car went through the rail—all the plans we made sitting in the office. The next thing he knew, he was there at his desk. But instead of going backward, he went forward nine months. And when he woke up in his office, my world changed too. That's the way it is with fellow travelers. We always know when a timeline changes."

"That's why I knew when you went back this morning," Alana said.

"Right! Like I said before, it means you're a traveler too."

"I'm okay with that, little sister." Alana seemed pleased. "Get to the part about bringing me back."

"Are you sure?" Nova laughed. "We can talk about it later if you want."

Alana grinned. "Don't make me hurt you!"

"Okay. After I confronted Dad, we decided to go to Willow Hill to talk to Aunt Jean about traveling.

"Aunt Jean was alive then?" asked Alana, obviously confused.

"We'll talk about that later, but yes. She was amazing. She told us how to do it—switch timelines. She even had me practice. Afterward, I was sure I could get you back. So one night when everyone else was on the porch, I came upstairs and traveled. That's when you came back."

"How'd you do it?"

"I pictured you with me on our sixteenth birthday. It wasn't that hard. I focused on you and it happened. It's like aiming a gun. That's what Aunt Jean said. You feel yourself honing in on the target, where you want to go. At first you feel like you're floating. Then you get sucked down a narrow tunnel. Unless you're just making a short jump, like this morning. Then it's more like a slight dip in the road."

"Weird."

"Yeah. I should've waited though. I wasn't ready."

"Why do you say that? I think you did pretty well. You brought me back, didn't you?"

"Yes, I did. I brought you back." Nova threw her arms around Alana and hugged her tightly.

After a minute, Alana pushed her away slightly and looked her in the eyes. "So why did you say you weren't ready?"

Nova tried to think of a plausible explanation for her careless remark, since she couldn't tell her sister about Marshall. She decided to keep it simple… and vague. "I just think it was reckless. I was lucky something bad didn't happen." *Like losing my little brother.*

Alana seemed satisfied with that explanation and eager to move on. "Okay. When can I learn to do this time traveling thing?" she asked excitedly. "I might want to go back and meet Jimi Hendrix."

"Really? Him?" Nova laughed. "I hate to disappoint you, but you can only travel in your own timeline, and when you do, you'll be the age you were at that time. That's why I couldn't go back in time to save you. I would have been a baby too. I had to go forward. Apparently Dad and I are the only ones who've done that. Well, that's not entirely true. If you go back to an event in your life, you can jump forward to the place you started as long as you don't wait too long. Aunt Jean called that a 'visit.' Others have done that. But traveling forward on its own… Dad and I are the only ones as far as Aunt Jean knew. So now I guess we've opened that door for everyone."

"How did you learn all of this? No! Wait a minute. How long ago was it that you traveled to bring me back? I mean, how long have I been alive?" Alana leaned forward and waited.

"You've been alive for sixteen years in your timeline. But from my perspective, it's only been…" Nova cleared her throat, stalling. How could she explain this to her sister?

"How long?"

"Six days, I guess. Since our birthday."

Alana sat there staring at Nova, white-faced. When she finally spoke, her voice sounded strained. "Six days? I've

only been alive six freaking days?" She seemed on the verge of losing control. "You've only known me that long?"

"Alana, you have a whole life behind you. Sixteen years! I just said that *to me* it feels like six days. So *I'm* the one who's messed up. Not you."

Alana relaxed a little. "Still. It's pretty weird, don't you think?"

"Absolutely. Very weird."

"So… am I what you expected?" Alana asked solemnly.

Nova smiled at her sister. "Yes and no."

"What does that mean?"

"I didn't have any real memories of you, so I guess I made you up years ago. I had an imaginary friend named Allie when I was little. I think deep down I expected you to be like her."

"And I'm not?" Alana seemed disappointed.

"No, you're not. You're better. Better than the Allie I created in my head and better than the sister I imagined." Nova smiled.

"You're pretty perfect too, little sister." Alana smiled, looking relieved. "But when I asked you if I'm what you expected you said yes and no. That was the no. What's the yes?"

Nova laughed. "You look almost exactly like I pictured."

"Like a Grant family traveler?" Alana grinned.

"Exactly."

"Well okay then!" Alana jumped up. "Let's do it! I want to try!"

"Now? Are you kidding?" Nova jumped up too. "It's not that easy!"

"You said Aunt Jean helped you practice. So you can help me. I want to see if I can do it too." Alana was clearly determined.

"Alana—"

"Allie," her sister corrected. "You've always called me Allie. I thought you'd been acting weird this past week because you were upset with me about something an that's why you started calling me Alana. At least now I know the real reason."

Nova tried to collect her thoughts. She didn't feel capable of teaching her sister how to travel safely. She barely knew how to herself, and she'd had Aunt Jean to help her. "*Allie*, I need to think about this a little bit, okay? Traveling is dangerous if you don't know what you're doing. You can't just decide to do it for fun. Too much can happen."

"Like what? David and I had a great time at Christina's party last week. Why couldn't I go back to that?"

"Because you wouldn't do things exactly the same. There would be small changes. And those small changes would affect other things, and those things would cause other changes. It's a ripple effect. You can change people's lives in ways you never meant to."

"But look at what you did! You brought me back and nothing bad happened," Alana pointed out.

Something bad did *happen*. She would never tell Alana about Marshall. She knew that now. What was the point? It was hard enough for Nova to live with his loss without dragging her sister along. "Trust me. Bad things can happen."

"I still want to try it. It's not fair to ask me not to. Can't you think of a way I can do it without messing anything up?" Alana couldn't be dissuaded.

"I'll make a deal with you," Nova said wearily. "I'll help you hop back a little tomorrow. That'll give me time to plan it. Okay?"

"I guess…" She was disappointed. "But you promise we'll do it tomorrow?"

"I promise. And I guess we should tell Dad I told you."

"Yes!" Alana perked up. "I can't wait to talk to him about it."

"Don't mention anything about practicing though. I guarantee you he won't go for that."

"Why not? Oh wait, I know what you're gonna to say. 'Trust me,' right?"

"Yeah." Nova laughed.

CHAPTER 17

The girls looked for Dayton, but he was nowhere in the house. Celeste was in their room, folding laundry with her hair up in a towel. She'd apparently showered after her run. Nova couldn't get over how beautiful she looked, happy and young.

"You look great, Mom," Nova said.

"I can't look great. But thank you, honey," she smiled, obviously pleased. "What are you girls doing?"

"Looking for Dad," Nova replied.

"He went to pick up a contract from Jason. Can I do something for you?"

"No, that's okay. I just… uh… wanted to show Allie some of the maps and things we got on our trip. I don't know what he did with them."

"He'll be back in a while. Why don't you two make some pancakes? You haven't had breakfast, have you?"

"No. Pancakes sound good," Alana said quickly, pulling Nova out the door and into the kitchen.

"What's the hurry? Oh yeah. You're starving." Nova said, laughing.

"Actually, I'm not anymore. I just thought of something," she whispered. "Does Ethan remember you dated before? And can I tell David?"

"No! He doesn't remember, and you can't tell anyone! That's really important," Nova said quietly. "It's hard to talk in here with Mom in her room. We need to go somewhere out of the house.”

Alana thought for a moment, then smiled. “Mom, we’re walking down to Trudy’s for breakfast.”

“All right,” Celeste answered. “Bring me back a chocolate chip muffin.”

“Sure, Mom,” Nova said as they walked out the back door.

Trudy’s was a little coffee shop next to the library. They had the best scones and muffins in town. The best part was that they played their background music a little too loud, so you could never hear what the people at the next table were saying.

As soon as they were sure they were out of earshot, Alana turned to Nova. “I can’t tell anyone? What about my husband? Years from now, when I have one?”

“I guess that’s up to you. The truth is, Ethan knew in the other timeline. It doesn’t matter now, because he’s not a traveler, so he doesn’t remember. Before I found out about traveling… all of it… I told him what I was going through. I told him I was in a different reality.”

“And he believed you?” Alana asked incredulously.

“Yes. It’s kind of a long story, but he did end up believing me.” Nova’s eyes filled with tears. “I don’t know how I would have gotten through it all if he hadn’t been with me. You can’t imagine what it was like waking up and finding Dad alive and everything changed.”

“You must have been so scared,” Alana said solemnly.

“I was. And then I was just confused. I had to figure out what had happened. When I finally confronted Dad, it was such a relief to get some answers.”

“So when he gets home, we’re telling him I know, right?” Alana asked.

“Right.”

“Okay then! We need carbs. Let’s get some scones!” She laughed.

Nova admired her sister’s ability to cope, no matter

what the circumstances. She wished she were more like that.

They made it to Trudy's and back in less than an hour. Dayton still wasn't home, so Nova decided to call Ethan. His mother picked up the phone.

"Hi, Mrs. MacGrady. This is Nova Grant. Is Ethan home?"

"Hello, Nova. Ethan's around here somewhere. Does he have your number? I can have him call you."

"He has it. Thanks, Mrs. MacGrady." Nova hung up the phone.

She'd made a decision while she was out with Alana. In spite of insisting that her sister keep this secret, she was planning tell Ethan everything. He'd been a source of support before, and she needed that now. After waiting a few minutes to see if he called back, she decided to go see him. This kind of conversation would be better in person anyway.

Alana was in her room, lying on her bed and looking deep in thought.

"I'm going over to Ethan's for a while since Dad's not back yet," Nova said. She wasn't sure if her sister heard her at first.

Then Alana turned and smiled. "I'm going over it all in my head and I have so many questions. I think I should write them all down."

"That's a good idea. You can show me when I get back. I won't be gone long," Nova assured her.

"Okay. I'll be here." Alana turned away, staring at the ceiling again.

Nova could imagine all that must be going through her head because she'd gone through the same thing. The only difference was that Nova hadn't needed to come to terms with being dead in previous timelines. She marveled at how well Alana was taking that fact.

She managed to slip out the back door without seeing Celeste. At this point, she didn't want to see anyone but Ethan. All the way to his house, she rehearsed her words over and over in her head, trying not to sound too crazy. The truth was no matter how she explained time travel, it sounded insane. It would be a miracle if he believed her.

Nova walked up the driveway as Ethan was coming out of his house.

"I was just coming to get you. How'd you know where I live?" he asked.

"That's an interesting story. Can we go inside?"

"Sure, hot girl." He grinned. "My parents had to run to the nursery to meet a delivery truck that was running late. So we have the house to ourselves."

"Don't get too excited. I want to talk. Actually, let's sit on the porch for a few minutes."

Ethan frowned. "This sounds serious. You're not breaking up with me already, are you?"

"No, but I do have something important to talk to you about."

"As long as we're not breaking up, shoot." He pulled two rocking chairs close to each other and motioned for her to sit. As soon as she did, he plopped down in the other one, pulled her legs into his lap, and started rubbing her ankles.

"Don't do that. I really need to talk to you."

"So talk," he laughed.

"I can't think with you doing that." Nova put her legs down and pushed her rocker back a little.

"Okay, hot girl." He scooted his chair closer.

"You're impossible."

"Yeah, I know. Now what's so important?"

She decided to dive right in. "Ethan, what would you do if you found out that time travel was possible? Not only that, but you had the ability to do it yourself?"

"Wow. Okay… I think I'd go back to see the signing of the Declaration of Independence, or maybe I'd meet Walt Disney while he was still young and poor so I could tell him to keep drawing the mouse and everything would work out." He laughed.

"Yeah, that's great. But what if you could only travel back and forth in your lifetime?"

Ethan smiled. "That's easy, hot girl. I'd go back and ask you out sooner."

Nova blushed. "You'd have to be sure you didn't do anything to change the outcome though. What if you went back and it changed other things? You'd have to be sure it was worth it, wouldn't you?"

"I guess so. Where's this going?"

"I wanted to know how you felt about the idea."

"Okay. It'd be cool. Are you hungry? Because I'm starved. Let's go to Burger Barn." He grabbed his keys out of his pocket and stood.

"Ethan! I'm not through!" Nova felt as if her heart was going to beat out of her chest. She had to tell him now or she'd never have the nerve.

"Jeez, what's going on?" Ethan frowned, dropping back into the rocker.

Nova took a deep breath. "This is gonna be hard to believe, but try, okay?"

"Yeah. Sure." Ethan leaned forward and gave her his full attention.

"My family… well, the Grant side… we can travel back and forth in our own timelines. Mostly they've all gone back in time to change a mistake. But my dad and I… we've gone forward too. I'm on the fourth timeline that I know about."

She waited for a reaction, but none came. Ethan was staring at her as though she'd sprouted antlers. For some reason, his expression reminded her of the time she walked into her health class and the teacher was passed out on the floor with Rodney, the student teacher, standing over him and looking just like Ethan was looking now. Nova managed not to give in to the inappropriate urge to laugh.

"Well? Ethan, say something."

"I'm not sure what to say. It's a weird joke."

"I'm not joking. I'll prove it. Your brother's name is Sam. It's his truck you're driving. You weren't supposed to get it until he left for school in August, but he got a job on campus and left early. Your birthday is June 2nd. Your dad goes to a flower show in Florida every summer, and your family owns a nursery. That's why you have so many flowers all the time, which you hate. You also hate pickles on your burgers, and your mom makes great oatmeal chocolate chip cookies. By the way, she used to clean your room all the time, but she lost it one day and told you that if you wanted to live in a sty that was your choice." She put her hand on his cheek.

"You call me 'hot girl' because a nova is an exploding star. And when you kiss me, you don't close your eyes until our lips touch. You were my boyfriend in my last timeline. You told me you loved me at my window the night before I left for Willow to see my aunt. While I was there, I traveled and brought Alana back. She has a heart condition and didn't live in my first three timelines. I switched to a timeline where she was alive, and that's where I am now. The problem is, my little brother is gone now. I woke up in this timeline and found out that he was never born. I have to fix it… get him back. I know this seems crazy and I don't blame you if you never want to see me again. But it's the truth. And there's one more thing…" Nova swallowed back tears. "I'm sorry I didn't tell you I love you that night at the window… because I do."

Ethan was staring at her with a shocked expression. Nova waited for him to say something. Finally she couldn't stand it any longer.

"Fine! I shouldn't have told you!" Nova jumped up, but Ethan grabbed her arm.

"Nova! Give me a minute, okay?" He stood there holding her arm for a moment before speaking again. "I just—I'll be right back. Stay here."

And with that, he left her on the porch, closing the door behind him. Nova felt hot tears running down her face. She had wanted so desperately for him to believe her. He must have thought she was delusional. Why would anyone believe such a crazy story? In his position, she would have had the same reaction. He was probably in there calling her parents right now.

Suddenly he was back. "Let's go inside."

"Why?"

"Just come in, okay?"

"Fine. We'll go to your room." She went around him into the house and down the hall to his room.

"How did you—?"

"I've been here before! That's how." She yanked open his bedroom door and froze. "Okay… this isn't what I expected." The room was mostly clean and orderly.

"What?" Ethan asked, confused.

"Your room is usually a lot messier than this."

"My mom comes in here and cleans up. I've told her a hundred times not to, but she still does it."

"Be glad she does."

"Nah, I wish she'd just leave it alone. How bad could it get?"

"Bad. Trust me." Nova laughed, but it sounded forced even to her. "By the way, where's Jack?"

Ethan stared at her, floored. "I put him in my parents' room so he wouldn't jump all over you."

"Go get him. I'll wait."

Ethan disappeared for a minute then came back with the dog, who bounded around the room a couple of times before claiming a spot on the bed. "How did you know about Jack?"

"I told you."

"Right. Okay, I'll take your word for it. So tell me about this time travel thing."

"You believe me?"

"Not exactly." He glanced at Jack. "Maybe, I guess."

"Wow. I figured you'd think I was out of my mind or something."

"Yeah, well… maybe you are. But just for argument's sake, let's go with it. When did you get here? I mean, this timeline? You said you got here and your brother was gone."

"It was on my birthday."

"So that's when you found out about your brother?"

"Yes."

"But we had such a great time that morning. How could you have been in such a good mood if you'd just found out your brother was gone?"

"I didn't know. I was excited to have Alana back. I didn't realize Marshall was gone until later."

"His name is Marshall?"

"Marshall Sheldon Grant. He just turned nine."

"That sucks. Sorry." After an awkward silence, he asked, "How'd you know all those things about me, like about Sam's truck?"

"You told me."

"Oh, right. I guess I told you all of it, huh?"

"Yeah, most of it. When we went to the Burger Barn on your birthday, I watched you pick all of the pickles off of your burger. That's the day you got your truck. You came by and picked me up and…"

"And what?"

"That was our best kiss. In the truck outside of the Burger Barn."

Ethan smiled at her. "Maybe that was the best *so far*."

Nova blushed. "Yeah. That was the best so far."

"And you knew where my house was and which one was my room and about Jack because you've been here before, in the other timeline."

"Right."

"Nova, I want to believe you because you obviously believe it. It's just not possible."

"Wait! I have my great-grandmother's journal!" She ran back to the porch and grabbed her bag off of the steps, where she'd dropped it, then returned to his room and sat on the bed. "She talks about traveling. You can read it yourself." Ethan took the diary and started reading. After what seemed like an hour, he laid it down and looked at her.

"Clearly your great-grandmother also believed she could time travel. That doesn't make it true."

"So you don't believe me."

"Why don't you tell me how we met… in the other life?"

"You sat beside me in the fifth grade and we became friends," she said sadly.

"We weren't in the same class in fifth grade."

Nova looked down at her hands. "Maybe not in this timeline, but in the last one we were. Then when we were in the eighth grade, we went on a field trip to Yale and you gave me a bracelet with a bulldog charm. I'd just gotten my braces off and you kissed me. After that, you were my boyfriend."

Ethan didn't say anything. When she looked up, she saw all the color had drained from his face.

"Ethan, what?"

"Oh my God… I used to see you every day in the hall that year when you went from English to math. I had a massive crush on you, but you never even looked at me. When we went to Yale, I made sure I got on your bus. I bought that bracelet at the gift shop, but I couldn't work up the nerve to give it to you." He walked over to the desk and pulled the bracelet out of the top drawer. "I guess better late than never." Ethan took her hand and slid the bracelet onto her wrist.

"Ethan…" Nova couldn't manage anything else.

He put his arms around her and pulled her close, kissing her tenderly. When he finally pulled back, tears were running down Nova's cheeks.

Ethan gently wiped them away. "You win, hot girl.

Holy crap… I believe you. What do we do now?"

"I don't know exactly." Nova couldn't get her thoughts in order with Ethan holding her.

"We could just keep doing this until you figure it out." He grinned.

"That would be great, but I eventually have to go home."

"Well, whatever you need, I'm in. I can't believe this. Talk about crazy! Not you. It's just… never mind. What did Alana say when you told her about Marshall?"

Nova looked down. "I haven't told her. I don't think I'm going to. What would be the point?"

"You don't think she'd want to know?" Ethan asked.

"I don't know. Maybe. But there's nothing she can do about it, so why lay that on her?"

"I guess you're right. If you told me something like that, that'd I caused my parents to lose another kid, I'd freak out. It's a pretty big secret to keep though. Well, not bigger than the whole time traveling thing."

"I told her about that."

"You did? What was her reaction?"

"She wants to try it." Nova shook her head. "I have a bad feeling about it though."

"Do you think I can do it too? Time travel, I mean?" Ethan asked eagerly.

"I don't know. Probably not. Most people can't, I guess. Non-travelers change too. They just don't know it. You've been in most of my timelines, maybe all of them. You just don't remember because you're not a traveler."

"That really sucks." He frowned. "I want to remember."

"Yeah. Sorry." Nova didn't know what else to say.

"Well, at least I know I'll always get the girl, right?"

He flashed the smile she knew so well, and she couldn't help herself. She threw her arms around him and kissed him, this time until they were both breathless. Nova finally pulled away.

"Nova, let's do it," he said excitedly.

"Excuse me?"

"No, not that. Time travel. Let's do it. I want to try."

Nova was completely rattled. "It's not that easy! I can't just do it on command!"

"Just go back in time, like, thirty minutes. I want to see if I can tell."

"There's no way I'm going back thirty minutes. I'd have to explain all of this all over again."

"Oh, okay." He pulled her beside him on the bed. "We'll sit here for a few minutes and you can travel back to now. One o'clock."

Jack crawled over and laid his head in Ethan's lap.

"Get down, buddy," Ethan said gently.

Jack jumped down and trotted out the door.

"Where's he going?" Nova asked, a little disappointed.

"He has a bed by the window in the den. Don't worry. He'll be back. So are we gonna do it?"

"I don't know. It would have to be more like 1:03, so I could be sure you'd remember." Nova looked at the clock again. It read 1:02. She wasn't at all sure that she wanted to travel at his house with him sitting next to her, but she was curious too.

"Come on, hot girl! What can it hurt?"

"You won't realize I've traveled, so what's the point?"

"Well... can't you change something? Maybe we could be back on the porch or at your house or something like that."

"It doesn't work that way. I mean, sometimes it does... oh whatever. Fine. We'll wait five minutes, then I'll go back to this exact moment... hopefully." She let out a nervous giggle.

"Five minutes. Then you'll do it?"

"You won't know."

"Maybe I will." He grinned. "So we're waiting five minutes."

"Four now."

"It'll be boring just sitting here. Let's see... what could we do that would make the time go by faster?" He scooted around until he was facing her.

"Ethan, I'm not making out with you for four minutes."

"Three." He took her face in his hands as he leaned forward and gently kissed her on the forehead, then the cheek. Finally he kissed her softly on the lips.

"I can't focus with you doing that." Nova's heart was pounding.

"Okay, hot girl, I'll stop. But only until you do it." He sat back slightly and smiled.

She was completely flustered. "Don't talk to me for a few minutes while I concentrate. This might not work, you know." She leaned back against the pillows on his bed and closed her eyes, trying to relax with him watching her. *This isn't going to work.*

Suddenly, Jack barked in the other room. Nova sat up and looked at the clock. It was 1:07.

"It's okay. He probably heard a leaf fall or something." Ethan was anxious to get on with it.

"I have an idea," Nova said, smiling.

She lay back against the pillows again, cleared her mind and focused. Even with the dog barking, it was surprisingly easy to feel herself drifting into that familiar place. She pictured the time on the clock—1:05. Within a few moments, she felt the familiar floating sensation and the slight drop. Nova's eyes flew open and she was there, staring into Ethan's eyes. She glanced at the clock and smiled. 1:05.

"Are we gonna do it?" Ethan asked, oblivious to the fact that they already had.

Nova was surprisingly disappointed. In spite of the odds against it, she realized that she had hoped he would know she'd traveled. "I just did."

"Really?" Ethan's face fell. "I thought I'd be able to tell something."

"I told you you wouldn't."

"How do I know you're not messing with me?"

Nova grinned. "Jack will start barking at 1:07."

"What?"

"Trust me."

They both looked at the clock. At precisely 1:07, Jack

barked.

Ethan looked at her in awe. "Oh, man! I thought you were nuts! I didn't think you could really… let's do it again!"

"I can't do it again! I have to go home."

"Seriously? Now?"

"Yes, now. I'm sorry."

"You can't stay a little longer? Please?"

"I need to go home. Alana and I have to talk to my dad."

"This is amazing! So your dad isn't just some guy who writes science fiction—he's the real thing."

"I'm glad you're so impressed."

"Yeah, I guess I am. If you're really going, I'll walk you." He rubbed his stomach. "But I might throw up on the way. Just so you know."

"What's wrong?"

"I'm kinda sick to my stomach. Excitement, I guess."

Nova was floored. "You are? Since when?"

"Since now. It's okay. If I have to puke, I won't do it in your yard." He attempted a feeble grin.

"Ethan…" Nova's mind was reeling. Only fellow travelers were supposed to be affected when someone close to them switched timelines. What had Aunt Jean said? It was like getting carsick. So why was Ethan feeling it?

He was staring at her. "What?"

"Nothing. It's not important," Nova lied. "I really need to get home."

"Let's go then, hot girl." He took her hand and didn't let it go until they reached her backyard.

"This may sound strange, but I'm going in through my window. I need some time alone, and Alana's probably waiting to pounce on me."

"Nothing you do surprises me anymore," Ethan said.

They walked around the side of the house. Nova pushed up the window and climbed inside.

"Nova," he whispered, careful not to alert anyone else in the house, "I'm feeling better. Now's your chance."

Nova was confused. "What?"

"Remember what you said you wished you'd done before… at the window?"

Nova didn't understand at first. Then she knew. It didn't matter that she'd only known him a short while in this timeline. He was the same Ethan—*her Ethan.* No amount of traveling would ever change that.

She leaned forward, inches from his face, and said softly, "I love you, Ethan," before putting her arms around his neck and kissing him tenderly.

CHAPTER 18

Alana burst into the room as Nova was closing the window. "Nice try, little sister. You didn't think I'd hear you coming in the window? What did he say when you told him?"

Nova could feel her face turning red. "What makes you think I told him?"

"Oh please. It was obvious you were going to. You're so easy to read. It's probably the whole twin thing. So what did he say?" Alana flopped on the bed and waited. "I'm not budging until you tell me."

"Okay, fine. He was great about it. Just like before. It's amazing really. It took a lot longer in the other timeline to convince him I wasn't delusional. I don't know if I'd be able to believe it if the situation was reversed and Ethan was trying to convince me that he could travel in time."

"So how did you? Convince him, I mean." Alana leaned forward, waiting anxiously.

This whole thing is an adventure to her. "It was the bracelet."

"What bracelet?"

Nova held up her hand and showed her sister the bracelet from Yale. "This one."

"Okay… that makes no sense. He gave you a bracelet with a dog charm and that made him believe?"

"It's kind of a long story. He bought it when we were at Yale in eighth grade but couldn't work up the nerve to give it to me. So when I knew about it, that convinced him." Nova realized she wasn't explaining it very well. "He bought it but never gave it to me in this timeline, but in the last one he did. He gave it to me on the field trip and that's when we started dating. When I told him that, he took it from his desk drawer where it's been since the eighth grade. There's no way I could have known about it unless he really did give it to me in another timeline."

Alana said nothing. She just sat there, leaning forward, with her lips pressed together and an odd expression, obviously trying to make sense of what she'd just heard.

"Allie, you look like you just swallowed a bug." Nova laughed.

"Very funny. I'm trying to decide if my brain can process what you just told me. I think I get it."

"Do you want me to say it again?" Nova offered.

"Oh my God, please don't. Besides, I don't think it'll make any difference."

"There was also the dog barking thing."

"What dog barking thing?"

"Never mind. He's a believer. Let's leave it at that."

"Okay." Alana lay back on the bed, smiling. "It's pretty cool, isn't it?"

"Yes, it is. By the way, I think you're doing great with all of this."

"Thanks, little sister," Alana seemed pleased. "So does Ethan know I'm a traveler too?"

"Yes, but you still can't tell David. It might not seem fair, but Ethan's different. I have a history with him, and it's hard to explain, but I feel like he's *supposed* to know."

"I hate to point out the obvious, but you don't have any more history with Ethan than you have with me."

"Okay, but I knew him in the other timeline. So that's history… sort of."

"Whatever you say. Don't worry. I'm not planning to tell David. He already thinks I'm crazy, so he'd never believe it anyway." Alana jumped up. "I'm ready, so let's do it!"

"Do what?" Nova asked warily, even though she knew exactly what her sister wanted to do.

Alana grabbed her arm excitedly. "Travel of course! I want to see if I can. We don't have to do something major. I just want to try." Alana wasn't kidding. She was obviously determined.

"Maybe we should wait until we talk to Dad."

Even as she said it, Nova knew her sister wouldn't wait. Alana was ready to jump in, just like she had that day at the pool when they were five years old. Dayton had said that Nova was afraid but not Alana. She was always ready to try something new. In the short time that Nova had known her sister, she'd already figured out that Alana's basic reaction to life was to jump first and think about it later.

"How about it? Will you show me how to travel?" Alana asked impatiently.

Nova gave in. "Okay, fine. But you have to do exactly as I say and no more. Deal?"

"Deal! What do I do?"

"You have to put yourself into a meditative state."

Alana frowned a little. "I don't know how to do that."

"It's not really that hard. You lie down and try to totally relax. You can start at your toes and go up if that helps."

Alana giggled. "You mean like we did when we were kids? Relax your toes, relax your feet, relax your ankles, relax your calves…"

"Yes, if that helps." Nova smiled. She was excited to be the teacher for a change.

"Okay. Once I get up to my head, then what?"

"You take long, slow breaths, in and out, until it becomes natural to breathe that way."

"Got it. Then what?"

"I'm not gonna fly through it. Just listen to my voice and do what I say without all the commentary."

"Okay. Sorry."

"Slow your thoughts." Nova worried that Alana's natural impatience could keep this from working. "Your mind can't run a hundred miles an hour or you'll never be relaxed and focused. Just listen to what I say without thinking of what's coming next."

"Sorry. I'll try to slow down, and I won't think ahead. Just be in the moment, right?"

"Right."

Alana closed her eyes again and breathed slowly, in and out.

Nova waited a few minutes before going on. "Next, what works for me is finding a sound to focus on. Aunt Jean didn't say to do that, but it helps me shut out everything else. That's important. Don't think about anything going on around you. When I'm getting ready to travel, I block out everything but that one sound."

Alana lay perfectly still with her eyes closed, breathing deeply. Nova watched her for another minute, then continued again.

"Take slow, deep breaths," Nova said, keeping her voice low and even as Aunt Jean had done when they'd practiced in the garden. She waited until Alana's breathing had slowed down and become rhythmic. "Now, think of something that happened in the last few minutes. A specific moment."

"Like when I walked in and saw you close the window?" Alana whispered without opening her eyes.

"That's perfect," Nova kept her voice low.

Alana's brow furrowed a little. "I can't find a noise to focus on. Does that matter?"

"Probably not. That's just something I do." It dawned

on her that she hadn't had a sound to latch onto at Ethan's.

She'd been able to travel without it, even with Jack barking.

She returned her attention to her sister. "You can do

what works for you. Just clear your mind and focus on the moment you want to travel to. Don't think about anything else. That's the most important thing. Don't let your mind wander at all or you could end up somewhere else, somewhere you don't want to be."

"Okay, I'm thinking of that moment," Alana said softly.

"Keep breathing slowly. Block out everything except the moment you want to travel to. You have to aim for that spot like you're looking through the scope of a rifle. Aunt Jean compared it to firing a gun at an object, except your object is a place on your timeline. Zero in on it. That exact spot. When it happens, you'll feel yourself floating. If you're just going a short distance on your timeline, there will be a sensation like a dip in the road when you travel. If you're going further backward or forward, it feels like you're being pulled through a tunnel. You're just traveling a few minutes, so—"

"A dip in the road, right?" Alana whispered.

"Right."

"Good. I'm not excited about a creepy underground tunnel."

"I didn't say it was underground."

"So it's not?"

Nova thought for a moment. "I guess it could be."

"Great."

"Are you doing this or what?"

"Sorry." Alana continued to lie perfectly still, breathing slowly and deliberately. After five or ten minutes, she looked as if she was asleep, except for the fact that every now and then she moved slightly, as though she was trying to get more comfortable. Nova realized that she hadn't experienced traveling from this perspective, and the thought of doing that was thrilling. She'd never really thought about what it would be like to watch someone travel. She stared at her sister, anxiously waiting.

Several more minutes passed and nothing happened.

She was tempted to touch Alana's shoulder, just to see if she had actually fallen asleep. And then suddenly Nova was kissing Ethan at the window, her arms around his neck.

"Hey, you two! Get a room!" Alana laughed as she burst in on them.

Nova jerked back inside. "Oh my God, Alana!"

She turned back to Ethan, who looked as though he wanted to drop in a hole. He had backed up a couple of steps and was peering over Nova's shoulder at an elated Alana.

"Ethan—" All of a sudden, Nova was out of breath. "I'm sorry about my crazy sister. I'll call you later."

Ethan nodded awkwardly, turned, and jogged off toward his house.

Nova turned on Alana. "That was so embarrassing! If you ever do that again, I'll stalk you and David everywhere you go. And I'm bringing my Polaroid!"

"Jeez, lighten up. I won't do it again." Alana giggled. "I just wanted to see you two make out. Nice job by the way."

"Have you ever heard the term 'personal space'? Because you're seriously in mine!"

"Okay, I get it. I wish you could've seen the look on your face though." Alana laughed. "Definitely worth it."

"Yeah? Well, thanks a lot for blowing a tender moment. How'd you do that, by the way? You weren't in the room when I kissed him before."

"I went back to the hall outside your room. The other time, I listened at the door for a minute. This time I didn't." Alana grinned.

"Thanks a lot."

"Okay, I'm sorry. Don't be mad."

"I'm not mad. I can always do a repeat performance." Nova smiled, thinking about traveling back to the kiss over and over.

"Oh my God. You're pathetic." Alana puckered her lips and made a kissing sound.

"Okay, stop. Dad's home. Let's go talk to him." Nova

lowered her voice. "But don't tell him you traveled, okay?"

"It'll be our secret." Alana winked as she flitted out the door.

Nova shook her head and smiled. "My sister's a traveler. God help us."

CHAPTER 19

Dayton was leaning back in the leather chair at his desk, his eyes closed. He seemed to be asleep. Nova was tempted to back out of the room, but Alana closed the door and the noise woke him.

Dayton leaned forward and put his arms on the desk. "What's up? You two look like you have something on your minds." His voice had an underlying tension.

Nova spoke before Alana could. "I talked to Alana about everything."

"Everything?"

Nova shot him a warning look that she hoped said, *except Marshall.* She continued before he could say anything else. "I told her about the Grants' ability to travel in time… and about your accident, and how *Mom and I* had such a hard time when you were gone. Allie knows about being, uh…"

"I think 'dead' is the word you're looking for, little sister," Alana blurted.

Dayton sat straight up in his chair. "I thought we were going to tell her together." He didn't really sound mad. He sounded relieved.

"The time seemed right, so I just did it," Nova answered, certain now that Dayton didn't mind her talking to her sister without him. He had never liked confrontation.

Dayton looked at Alana. "What do you think about all of this, honey?"

"I'm good with it." She beamed.

"You are? Just like that?" Dayton asked

incredulously.

She nodded vigorously. "Actually, the more I think about it, the better it gets. I'll never fail another test. And don't even get me started on winning the lottery. I'll just have to figure out where I want to spend all that money." She rubbed her chin as though she was mulling over the possibilities.

Dayton frowned. "Now wait! That's not what we do. You can't just travel on a whim. And we've never used it to gamble. It's a powerful and potentially dangerous ability."

"Dad!" Alana laughed. "I'm kidding. I understand it's a big deal, okay?"

"Okay. You had me scared there for a minute." His posture relaxed a little. "It's just that the Grants have always tried to use this gift for good. Our power to change events affects everyone around us, not just our family. We've always believed there was a reason we were given the ability, rather than someone like Hitler or Stalin. Do you understand?"

"Sure." Alana looked at Nova and winked.

Dayton sighed and shook his head. "Don't make us regret telling you, Allie."

"I won't." This time, Alana obviously meant it. "And I won't tell anyone else even though Nova told Ethan."

Nova's mouth flew open. So much for sisterly trust.

Dayton looked at Nova, frowning. "You told Ethan again? Why on earth did you do that?"

"I don't know. I—I just did it." Nova felt tongue-tied. She should have cleared it with her dad first. "I'm sorry."

"Well, what's done is done. But please don't tell anyone else, either of you." He looked pointedly at Nova. "Understand?"

"Sure, Dad," Alana answered quickly for both of them. She grinned at Nova. "So now I'm the good daughter. If you'd actually been around these past sixteen years, you'd know how weird that is."

"I think I can figure it out." Nova gave her a wry

smile.

Alana turned back to Dayton. "I have, like, a jillion questions. Where did this gift come from? And is it only us? I mean, the Grants?"

"No one knows where it came from, but our family has had it for as long as anyone can remember. And as far as anyone else having the same ability, we don't know. We've never met any other travelers but probably wouldn't know it even if we did. It does seem logical that others would be able to do it though."

"So we could be passing other travelers on the street and never know it?"

"That's possible, yes."

"Wow…" Alana jumped onto Dayton's desk and sat. "How did we end up in New England if most of the family is in the Carolinas?"

"Let's see." Dayton leaned back in his chair, thinking. "Your great-great-grandfather, William Grant, was from Ohio. He met Lily Mitchell when he was in Charleston on business sometime in the late 1800s. Some of my information came from Aunt Jean and Uncle Bill when I was young, before we stopped going to visit them. Then Mother told me some things about the family right before I went to college. From what I can remember, Lily didn't want to leave her family and would only agree to marry William if he'd move down there. So that's how so many of the Grants ended up in the South."

"Could most of those Grants time travel?" Alana was hanging on his every word.

"I guess so," Dayton answered. "There were those who couldn't, like Uncle Bill's son, Michael. But I think most of them could."

"Did they travel a lot? I meant, as far as you know?"

"I have no idea, honey. I assume they must have sometimes, but I think mostly they just lived their lives."

"But what's the point of having this amazing gift if you don't use it? Couldn't we, I don't know… prevent people from walking in front of cars, or stop a train from derailing, or a fire from starting? It seems like you could travel every day to stop all kinds of bad things from happening. You'd read the paper about some kid who got hit riding his bike and you'd go back and warn him. If there were enough of us, we could basically save the world—stop wars, prevent outbreaks of diseases, stop crazy dictators from launching nuclear weapons, keep tsunamis from killing thousands of people…"

"Like superheroes?" he asked, apparently amused.

"Exactly!" she exclaimed. "We could be superheroes for real!"

Dayton shook his head. "I'm sure it seems like you could constantly save people with this gift, but you can't. It takes something out of you every time you travel, even if you can't tell at first. And interfering with other lives, even with the best intentions, doesn't always turn out the way you mean for it to. You have to be very careful where you chose to get involved. You might stop an accident only to have something else happen as a result. It's the ripple effect. I remember Aunt Jean arguing with Uncle Bill about that when I was little. I don't know the details, but Aunt Jean was saying that the drunk driver they stopped from hitting the kid two houses down went on to kill someone else a week later. The kid would have been in the hospital, but he would have recovered and the guy would have been in jail. Instead, he killed a pregnant woman crossing the street. I don't know what they ended up doing, whether or not they went back again to change it, but I'll never forget hearing them talk about it. That was when we were down south visiting them, right before my mother had her big argument with Aunt Jean that broke us off from the family for good."

"You never told me that story," Nova said sadly. "I wish you knew what happened to the woman. I hope they went back again and saved her."

"Me too, honey." Dayton looked her in the eyes, and Nova understood. If things worked out the way they hoped, they'd ask Aunt Jean about it in person.

"Why haven't you told Mom about traveling?" Alana pressed. "If I were her, I'd want to know."

"I suppose I never told her because that's the way it's always been. No one knew except those of us who could travel. Honestly, I don't see the point in talking to her about this. She probably wouldn't believe me. She'd think I'd written one too many science fiction stories."

"Yeah, I guess you're right. If Nova hadn't traveled to show me, I wouldn't have believed her either. And then she showed me how to do it and I—" Alana stopped suddenly, then jerked around and mouthed "I'm sorry" to a stunned Nova.

Several seconds passed in complete silence before Dayton jumped up from his chair and turned on Nova. "You what?"

"Dad, she didn't believe me." Nova said quickly. "So I went back about five or ten minutes. That's all. She was in the den when I did it."

"That's not what I mean and you know it. You showed your sister how to travel?"

"Yeah." Nova looked at the floor.

"Why did you do that? You know how dangerous it is! What if she'd changed something that couldn't be fixed?"

Nova started to say, "Like I did?" but she bit her tongue.

"Look, I don't want you, *either of you,* traveling anymore without talking to me," he said emphatically. "It sounds like you've been reckless, Nova."

Nova could tell he wanted to add "again." She started to say that he needed to stop leaving everything up to her if he didn't like the way she did things, but again bit her tongue. There was no reason to start a fight. It wouldn't matter soon anyway, because one way or another, she intended to switch to another timeline.

"When did you girls do this?" he demanded.

"Just before we came in here. I guess you slept

through it."

"Yeah. I guess so." He was still fuming.

Celeste opened the office door. "What's going on in here?"

"We're talking about the book," Dayton lied.

"Well, I have lunch laid out if anyone's hungry."

"We're coming, babe." Dayton forced a smile. As soon as she disappeared up the hallway, he looked at both of his girls, no trace of the smile left. "Do we understand each other? No more traveling without talking it out first?"

"We understand," Nova answered.

Both girls followed Dayton out of the office, but Alana caught Nova's arm before they got to the kitchen. She leaned in and whispered in Nova's ear, "Dad seems a little tense. Was he like that before? In the other timeline?"

"Not really. I always thought he acted like a big kid," Nova responded softly.

"Yeah, that describes the dad I know too—a big kid. Why is he so different?" she asked.

"I don't know," Nova answered.

But the truth was she knew exactly why he was different. He'd lost his son just days before. Pretending everything was normal in spite of this new harsh reality was taking its toll. Sooner or later, Nova or Dayton would crack, and that would be the end of normalcy. Nova hoped that she'd come up with a plan and travel before that happened.

"What are you girls doing?" Celeste motioned for them to come on. "I have sliced turkey and roast beef out for sandwiches. *And* I made a pitcher of sweet tea." She sounded very pleased with herself.

Nova pulled her chair back, noticing again that there was no chip. She ran her hand along the rim, thinking of Marshall. The lunch, the sweet tea—all of it—reminded Nova of a lunch Aunt Jean would have set out, and she started to tear up right there at the table. Aunt Jean and Marshall… both gone. Nova shook herself mentally, coming back to the present as Celeste poured tea into a glass and set it at her place. Dayton took a big gulp from his glass and choked, coughing up half of it.

"Good heavens, Day!" Celeste laughed.

"Wow, swallowed too much! You know how I love this stuff. Once a Southern boy, always a Southern boy," he managed to get out.

"You barely lived in the South. Your mother moved you up here when you were what, a year old? And you didn't visit your family but a few times," Celeste pointed out.

"It's in the genes, honey." Dayton laughed, but Nova thought it sounded forced.

"That must be why—" Nova caught herself. She'd almost said that must be why Marshall loved sweet tea too. She couldn't let herself slip like that! How would she explain who Marshall was to Celeste and Alana? She stuffed the rest of her sandwich in her mouth and took a gulp of tea, nearly choking as well.

"Nova, not you too!" her mother scolded. "What's happened to your table manners?"

"Sorry, Mom," Nova managed.

She stood and rinsed her plate, then stuck it in the dishwasher before taking off down the hall to her room. Once inside, she closed her door and leaned against it. Every time she started to feel at home in this timeline, something happened to remind her of her little brother, and the massive guilt nearly crushed her. She lay on her bed and let the tears come. They were no closer to figuring out how to bring Marshall back than they had been when they'd first realized he was gone. *What are we gonna do, Aunt Jean?*

She wished her aunt was sitting there on the bed beside her. Maybe she should visit her again. It had worked out the first time. Maybe now that she had the journal, Aunt Jean could help her decipher it.

Nova sat up, thinking. She could do it now, before anyone came looking for her. Excited about the prospect of going back to Willow Hill and seeing her aunt again, she jumped up and tiptoed to her door. She could hear them all still talking in the kitchen, so she pushed the door closed and locked it.

CHAPTER 20

Nova lay on her bed and closed her eyes, breathing slowly and rhythmically. There was no specific sound to latch onto, but she'd already seen that she didn't need it.

She took another deep breath and blocked everything out except the image of Aunt Jean in the kitchen that morning. She'd go back to the exact spot in time that she'd visited before. She allowed her mind to slowly form the scene, every detail the same as before. It was surprisingly easy. She focused on that image, the moment she had seen Aunt Jean pulling the tray of muffins out of the oven. The floating sensation came swiftly—just as Nova's mind wandered to when Alana had nearly caught her when she traveled back the last time. She could hear her sister banging on the door.

Nova tried to refocus on Aunt Jean, but it was too late. She felt her body tense just before it was yanked violently through the tunnel. She woke up in the four-poster at Willow Hill, and Alana was pounding on the door.

"Nova, why is your door locked? Open up! Aunt Jean's down there cooking."

Nova jerked out of bed, trying to catch her breath. *Oh my God! What did I do wrong?* The knocking stopped for a moment, then resumed.

"I heard you get out of bed! Open up. I'm not leaving." Alana was obviously determined to wait her out.

Nova's heart was racing. The first time she'd done

this, Alana had come to the door as she was *leaving,* not when she arrived. It must be at least fifteen minutes later than her other visit. She couldn't be sure exactly. How was she supposed to talk to Aunt Jean now?

"Open up. I hear you in there." Alana wiggled the knob.

She would have to do something. She needed to see Aunt Jean, and apparently the only way she'd be able to do that was to go through Alana. *I'll just have to deal with her.* She walked over and unlocked the door.

Her sister burst in immediately. "Jeez, what the heck? Why didn't you open the door?"

"Sorry. I-I don't know. I was still half asleep, I guess."

"You look weird. Are you okay?" Alana asked.

"I'm fine. Why don't you go to breakfast? I'll be there in a minute." Nova needed to collect herself, and that would be hard with Alana flitting around and talking nonstop.

"Nah. I'll wait." Alana jumped up on the bed and crossed her legs.

Nova studied her sister. Alana looked basically the same, except for the fact that her hair was a little longer and she looked very slightly younger. Curious about her own looks, Nova stepped into the bathroom and peered into the mirror. Her hair was in a loose ponytail that had turned into a bird's nest overnight, but other than that she seemed the same. Except for one thing.

She leaned in closer to the mirror and gasped. "Why is my freaking nose pierced?"

Alana burst out laughing. "I told you you'd end up hating it! You'll never catch me punching holes in *my* face!"

"Oh my God…" Nova tugged on the tiny stud.

"Ouch! It hurts!"

"That's because you keep taking it out and putting it back in. Like that's really fooling anyone. Aunt Jean said something about it the first day we were here."

"I can't believe I let somebody shove a needle through my nose. It's ridiculous."

"Like I said, little sister, told ya!"

Alana laughed, but Nova saw no humor in the situation. Why did she have a pierced nostril now but not a year from now? What would have possessed her to do this?

"*Never* do something permanent to please a guy, especially one like Steven. He's such a jerk. Honestly, why do you like him?" Alana kept chattering away, not waiting for an answer. "Aunt Jean says it'll probably get infected with you hanging out at the barn. No telling what kind of germs are floating around in all that hay and manure. As a matter of fact, it looks a little red right now." She jumped down from the bed and came over, then leaned in close, squinting. "Yep. Definitely red."

"I'll fix that right now." Nova undid the clasp in her nostril and slid out the stud, feeling as though she could be sick any moment. Then she dropped it in the trash can. "There. No more pierced nose."

There was a tiny red spot where the stud used to be, but she figured it would heal and no one would ever know it had been there. Grabbing a bar of soap from the tub, she lathered her face before rinsing it off at the sink. The spot was still red and a little sore.

"I hope I'm not scarred for life," she complained.

"You're a dork, you know that?" Alana laughed.

"Yeah, I know." A split second later, an adrenaline rush hit her when she realized that she'd let precious time pass. She turned to Alana. "Go on down and tell Aunt Jean I'll be there in a sec. I want to change." When Alana didn't move, Nova shouted, "Go!"

"Okay, lighten up." Alana took off down the hall, still laughing.

Nova stared at herself in the mirror, then closed her eyes and allowed her brain to settle down. The connection was still there, but she'd need to hurry. She pulled on a pair of shorts that were crumpled on the floor next to her bed.

They had a grass stain on them, but she wasn't about to take the time to find clean ones. She wouldn't be here that long.

She took off down the hallway, descended the stairs two at a time, and burst into the kitchen out of breath. Aunt Jean was pouring orange juice into a glass for Alana.

"Well, there you are! My goodness, rough night?" Aunt Jean laughed.

"Yeah, sort of… I guess. Aunt Jean, can I talk to you, uh, privately?" Nova sputtered.

Aunt Jean stopped laughing, suddenly alert. "Why sure, honey." She set the juice in front of Alana, who was looking at Nova suspiciously.

"What's your deal this morning?" Alana asked.

"Nothing… I'll tell you later. I just need Aunt Jean for a minute."

Frowning slightly, Aunt Jean motioned for Nova to follow her out onto the veranda. "Will this do, honey?"

"Can we go to the gazebo?" Nova wanted to make sure they weren't overheard.

"Of course we can." Aunt Jean took off briskly down the path.

Nova's feet made a crunching sound on the pebble path as she followed her through the garden. The sound of the horses drifted up from the barn. They were snorting and stomping their feet, anxious for their breakfast. Justin was probably throwing hay down the chutes. Marshall had loved feeding the horses. She felt a fresh pain in the pit of her stomach.

Time seemed to stand still out here among the flowers. There was still something magical about it. She allowed herself to hope that this time they'd figure it all out. Aunt Jean would read Evelyn's journal and a light would go off in her head.

As soon as they climbed the steps into the gazebo and sat in the wicker chairs, Aunt Jean leaned toward her and looked her in the eyes. "You came back, didn't you?"

Nova threw her arms around her aunt and hugged her

tightly before letting go and sitting back. "I had to! So much has happened since I was here before."

"Is that a fact?"

"Yes! I needed to talk to you again."

"Just a minute, honey. Can you still feel the connection?"

Nova closed her eyes. It was still there, hardly faded at all. "Yes, I can."

"All right then, make it quick."

"I found Evelyn's journal. It's incredible, full of information. But she talks about things I don't understand."

"For instance?" Aunt Jean's face wore an intense expression.

"Like using someone else's timeline to change yours. I don't understand how to do that. And would that even be possible as far as Marshall is concerned? She also talks about powers that haven't been realized. What does she mean?"

"I'm not sure. What else did she write in her journal?" Aunt Jean asked.

"Can't we just go get it? We can read it together until I have to go back." Nova jumped up, but Aunt Jean took her arm and directed her to sit down again.

"I have to find it," her aunt said.

"But it's in the chest! I found it... or I *will* find it, taped underneath the last drawer from the bottom!"

"Well, at least now I know where to put it." Aunt Jean chuckled, shaking her head. "Right after you visited before, I remembered something. We had a friend of Justin's staying in that room while they were in their last year of college in Charlotte. I cleaned out the chest so he could use it. I can't remember what I did with Mother's journal. My plan was to look for it and put it back in the chest before you'd be here next summer to find it. You haven't given me time to do that. It's been less than a half an hour since your first visit."

"No! I can't believe I've done this for nothing!" Nova was in tears. "I really need your help."

"I know, but there's something else. You can't keep coming back to the same place in time."

"What do you mean?" Nova asked. "I came back here with no trouble."

"But you didn't land in the exact same moment, even though I bet you tried, did you?"

Nova thought about that. "I guess not. I was a little later than before. But that's because I thought about Alana at the door right before I traveled. It was my fault I didn't come back to the same spot."

"That's what happens. Your mind won't let you land in the same moment. You'll always be off a little. And the more you try to hit that mark, the farther off you'll be."

"Why?"

"I don't know exactly. It's just the way it is." Aunt Jean sighed.

Nova shook her head. "That doesn't make sense."

Aunt Jean threw her head back and laughed. "I'll give you that! But tell me what part of any of this *does* make sense. Honestly, sometimes you just have to say, 'Okay, good to know,' and move on."

"I see your point," Nova replied, collapsing farther into the wicker chair.

"Listen, child, you don't want to keep traveling, using up your strength, just to have these short talks that don't get you anywhere. You can figure out what to do from the journal. I know you can. Mother always used to say, 'Don't make things complicated when they're really very simple.' Read what she wrote with that in mind. Now, close your eyes. Can you feel the tug back to your present?"

Nova closed her eyes. "It's getting weaker, but it's still there."

"Okay, then. Run along now," Aunt Jean said softly.

Nova opened her eyes and hesitated, looking back toward the house. Her parents must have come down for breakfast because she could hear Alana's laughter floating out into the garden and mixing with the sounds drifting up from the barn. It would be wonderful to experience Willow Hill with her sister.

"Why doesn't Alana know about traveling?" Nova asked quietly. "She can do it, you know. I've seen her."

"Up to now, there hasn't been a reason for her to know. Dayton hasn't traveled, so there's no time switch to notice. And we never travel when you're all down here, so neither of you girls have had the opportunity to find out. But it's kind of like the whole Santa Claus thing. Eventually, it all comes out."

"So in this timeline, I don't know yet either?" Nova asked.

"Why would you, honey? Alana didn't die from her heart condition. Your dad didn't have the accident on the bridge. He's had no reason to travel, so you've had no reason to notice anything amiss."

Nova continued to gaze back toward the house, listening to her sister's laughter. It was so tempting to stay put, to let the connection back to the present wither away.

"I know what you're thinking, honey. A whole year with your sister, doing all the things you missed out on. But you can't stay. After a year, the memory of Marshall would fade."

"I'd never forget him," Nova said softly.

"You don't think so now, but trust me. You'd get used to this timeline. You wouldn't be able to go back to the same place you were before. You'd become accustomed to life without him. That's what happened to Kate. Her memories of Daniel and the baby faded the longer she lived without them. If you don't go back now, you may never see your little brother again."

Nova turned back to her aunt. "Will I see you again?"

Aunt Jean smiled. "We'll see each other, honey."

"Promise?" Nova took her aunt's hand.

"I promise." Aunt Jean's eyes filled with tears. "Now go."

"They're all in the kitchen. I don't want to see them

right now."

"You don't have to. You can travel back from here. The connection isn't to a particular place. It's to you."

"But you told me to go back to my room last time."

"It helps to go back to the same place, especially when you first start traveling. It helps you focus. But as you get stronger, it's not necessary."

"Okay. I love you, Aunt Jean."

"I love you too, honey."

Nova closed her eyes again. As soon as she felt the fading connection, she grabbed hold of it and let it pull her back to the present. Opening her eyes again, she took in a deep breath. She was home.

CHAPTER 21

Nova lay on her bed, staring at the ceiling with tears welling up and spilling over, but she did nothing to stop them. Her little brother's whole life had been ahead of him when she'd snuffed it out. The least she could do was cry for him.

Alana tapped lightly on her door. "Let me in."

Nova had no desire to see anyone. Why couldn't her sister just leave her alone? She lay there quietly, not responding. Alana knocked again. As usual, she wasn't going to give up. Nova wiped her face with her shirt and unlocked the door before sitting on the bed again.

"What's going on?" Alana sat on the bed beside her and waited.

"Nothing."

Alana was quiet for a few moments, seeming to gather her thoughts. Finally she leaned forward and looked Nova in the eyes. "Do you think your personality changes from timeline to timeline?"

Nova was confused by the question, but she thought about it anyway then responded confidently. "No, I don't think it does. Because no matter what happens, you're still the same person."

"That's good to know." Alana smiled slightly. "Because something's wrong. I know you feel like you've only known me a week or so, but I've known you for sixteen years. I can tell when you're upset even when you try to hide it. So, little sister, what's eating at you?"

Nova was taken aback. "N-nothing. Maybe you can't read me as well as you think you can."

"Okay. Since you won't tell me, here's what I think. You've been different since our birthdays. So I think something changed when you traveled—something other than me being alive, that is. I think something happened you weren't expecting. Something bad."

"Nothing happened," Nova lied.

"Then you shouldn't have a problem telling me what life was like before."

"Life was good. I just wanted you to be here too." That was the truth.

"Where were you when you traveled?"

"At Willow Hill. In the guest room upstairs. I planned all day exactly how I was gonna do it," Nova said without thinking. "Aunt Jean must have known, because she came into my room and helped me."

"Why didn't you tell me?"

"I just… I didn't want you to feel bad." Nova realized she was just making it worse.

Alana's eyes filled with tears. "She died because of me?"

"No, of course not." Nova hoped she wasn't lying again. Keeping secrets from her sister was proving to be difficult.

"Then what happened to her?"

"I think she just got tired. She'd traveled a lot, and it wore her down. She told me that eventually you have to stop and let nature take its course."

"So she helped you, then she died. That sounds like it was because of me," Alana replied sadly.

"No, it wasn't. She died in a different timeline. She was just tired. She'd traveled a lot and that was it," Nova insisted.

"Is that all?" Alana clearly suspected that there was more to the story.

"What do you mean?"

"Is that the only change since you brought me back?" Alana sat there, waiting for an answer.

After a few moments, Nova said, "There are lots of little changes. I didn't know half the people at the party, so my friends are different. Dad's office used to be where your room is. Stuff like that."

"So the room next to yours was… what?" Alana asked.

"It was a… guest room," Nova lied.

"Oh." Alana frowned slightly. "What was it like around here when Dad was gone?"

"Honestly, I hate thinking about it," Nova answered, grateful to be able to tell the truth about something.

"I'm sure. But I really want to know."

"It was awful. Mom was really depressed. She kept dying her hair. Practically every couple of weeks it was a new color. You would hardly have recognized her. She never asked about school or cooked or laughed. We argued all the time." Nova frowned, remembering how hard it was not so long ago.

"I'm glad I missed that," Alana said. "I can't imagine Mom that way."

"Yeah… can I ask you a question?"

"Shoot, little sister." Alana smiled.

"What was I like before our birthday?"

Alana grinned. "Oh my God. You could be a pain in the ass! Always wanting to do the right thing, making straight As, never lying…"

Nova looked down at her hands. *I guess that much has changed.*

Alana laughed. "It annoyed the crap out of me sometimes. But you've always been my best friend. I knew I could always count on you. And we've had some great times, even if I did have to sometimes drag you along kicking and screaming!"

Nova was anxious to discover what life would have

been like with her twin sister. "Tell me."

"Do you remember when we were fourteen and we toilet-papered Josh Harrison's yard and his brother came out and chased us? Wait, what am I saying? Of course you don't remember. Anyway, he followed us back to our house and kept throwing rocks at the front door. I knew Mom and Dad would be home soon, so after a while, I went outside to talk to him. He said he'd forget all about it if we both kissed him."

"Eww!" Nova grimaced. "Like we'd really do that!"

"Yeah, I knew you wouldn't go for it. So I kissed him twice." Alana grinned.

"Please tell me you didn't kiss crazy Dean Harrison!"

"Yes, I did. He tried to stick his tongue down my throat and I bit it."

"I think I'm gonna be sick..." Nova was nearly rolling on the floor. "What happened after that?"

"We didn't get in trouble, but he followed me around at school for months. It was creepy. I finally told him to meet me behind the gym during lunch. When he showed up, I punched him in the stomach and told him the next time my aim would be lower. He got the message! I don't think he came within fifty feet of me after that!" Alana giggled. "Thank God he graduated last year."

"Tell me more things that happened. They don't all have to be gross though. Tell me about the picture of us on the pier."

"The one on the shelf in my room?"

"Yeah. How old were we?"

"About eight or nine, I think," Alana replied.

Marshall's age.

"Mom and Dad rented a cabin at Moosehead Lake in Maine for two weeks."

"Wow, I can't see Mom staying in a cabin for two weeks! She's not the camping type." Nova laughed.

"Oh no, this cabin was gorgeous! It had floor-to-ceiling windows, a gourmet kitchen, a big fireplace with leather chairs, and a huge deck right on the water. Our room had bunk beds and its own balcony. We took the pontoon out every day with a picnic. It was so much fun!" Alana was obviously enjoying the memory. "You and I used to sit on the deck with our feet in the water, and these little fish would come up and try to eat our toes!"

"That gives me chills just thinking about it!" Nova grimaced. "I wish I could remember. Did we ever go back?"

"That's the sad part. Mom and Dad promised we'd go back every year, but I think the owners sold the place or something. The next summer, Dad called the rental company and they said it wasn't for rent anymore. We have a bunch of pictures from the trip though."

Nova's face lit up. "I'd love to see pictures!" She hadn't even thought about the fact that there would be photos documenting her life growing up with her sister.

They spent the next two hours looking through albums and boxes loaded down with pictures. Every birthday, Christmas, and Easter had been thoroughly captured on film, and one thing was clear—Nova and Alana had been inseparable. No wonder Alana claimed to know her so well. They'd done everything together—every dance class, summer camp, swimming lesson, sleepover with friends, camp out, lemonade stand, vacation, field trip—all of it. Nova felt her heart breaking over the fact that she remembered none of it. Not one thing.

"What's wrong?" Alana nudged Nova's shoulder.

"All these pictures of us. I'm just… sad. I want to remember everything, but that's never gonna happen."

"I'll tell you whatever you want to know, in detail. It'll be like you were there too."

Nova managed a smile. "It won't be the same, but it'll help."

"Any time you want to talk, I'm always here for you. You know that, right?"

"I know. Thanks, Allie. The pictures are awesome. Maybe if we talk about them enough, they'll seem like my memories. Do you think that's possible?"

Alana laughed. "Little sister, I'm beginning to think *anything* is possible."

"Speaking of anything being possible, do you remember when I had my nose pierced?" Nova asked.

"Of course. Cro-Magnon Man made you do it." Alana wrinkled her nose.

"Who?"

"Steven. Living proof that looks aren't everything," Alana remarked. "It healed up nicely though." She leaned in for a closer look. "Yep. You can't even see where it was."

Nova made a mental note to figure out who Steven was so she could avoid him in the future. "He must have been a jerk."

"Duh," Alana agreed. "He told you you'd look hot with a pierced nose. Like you don't already?"

"Why did I even like him if he was such a loser?"

"He didn't seem like that at first. He was pretty nice. Brought you flowers and said 'yes, ma'am' and 'yes, sir' to Mom and Dad. I liked him too in the beginning. But then his coach made him starting quarterback and his head got big. It was all downhill from there."

"So he played football? I can't imagine falling for someone like that." Nova frowned.

Alana was studying her. "You don't even remember him, do you?"

"I'm afraid not." Nova shook her head.

"No worries, little sister. You're not missing anything. Ethan's so much better. Better looking and a lot nicer. He's a good guy."

"I know. I love him," Nova said honestly.

CHAPTER 22

Hours later, Nova lay in bed, unable to sleep, thinking about the memories from this life that she'd never share with her sister. No matter how many times she changed timelines, she'd never know what it was like to grow up with Alana.

That train of thought brought her around to Ethan and the fact that he had become nauseated briefly after she traveled at his house. If he'd felt the effects of traveling, did that mean he was also a traveler? Aunt Jean had mentioned that there could be others. Maybe the Grants weren't the only ones capable of changing timelines at will. Maybe they were just the ones to discover it and perfect it. Maybe other people whose gift wasn't developed could feel the change but chalked it up to déjà vu or a piece of spoiled fruit. She should have told Ethan that he was feeling the effects of jumping back and forth in his timeline, but it had unsettled her that he did. Dealing with the fact that the Grants could travel was hard enough without adding Ethan and the rest of the world to that scenario.

Nova still wanted to talk to Grandma Kate again, but she didn't want to go with her dad. He'd blown the first time pretty badly. Maybe Ethan would go with her! They just

needed to find an excuse to get away for the whole day. Nova picked up the phone and punched in his number. He picked up on the second ring.

"I was just thinking about my hot girlfriend."

"You know how you said you'd help me?"

"Sure. What can I do for you, hot girl?"

"You can take me to see my grandmother… in New Hampshire." Nova held her breath, waiting for some kind of response. He took so long to answer she wondered if she'd lost the connection. "Hello?"

"I'm here. I'm just thinking." Ethan sounded serious. "We'd be gone for a whole day. Even if we left early in the morning, we wouldn't be back until late. Are you sure you can do that?"

"I thought we'd come up with an excuse. Actually, I hoped *you'd* come up with one." Nova laughed nervously.

"I don't think my parents would agree to let me drive you into another state. I haven't had the truck that long. They'd be worried."

"Okay, never mind then. It was just an idea." Nova was crushed. She'd been sure he'd agree to go.

"Let me call you back in a few minutes, okay?"

"Okay."

Nova hung up, defeated. Lying on her bed, everything seemed hopeless. After a few minutes, she heard someone tapping on the window and she nearly jumped out of her skin.

"Ethan!" she whispered a little too loud as she raised the window. "Are you trying to kill me? I almost had a heart attack! Why didn't you tell me you were coming over?"

Ethan crawled in the window and put his arms around her, grinning. "I came up with a great idea."

"Oh yeah?" she asked, a little flustered from standing there in Ethan's arms as she wore only a T-shirt and boxers. "What's your great idea?"

"We go in the morning. Early. Your mom runs, right?"

"Yes, but Dad's here… and Alana."

"Tell them you're going with me to pick up some flowers for my parents' store and then we're making deliveries. That should give us until dinnertime at least. If we're later than that, you can call them and say we're going to a movie or something."

"You want to leave in the morning?" Nova was getting excited. Ethan's excuse could actually work. Alana wouldn't think of intruding on a daylong date with Ethan, and her parents had no reason to think she'd be lying. "Mom leaves by six thirty to run. Can you be here right after that?"

"Sure thing." Ethan kissed her. "Now I need to come up with an excuse *my* parents will buy. I can't tell them we're picking up plants and making deliveries."

"Oh yeah. Just tell them we're going to the library to do some research for my dad, then to Burger Barn and the mall. You could use the movie thing too."

"I'll figure something out." He smiled, obviously pleased at her reaction to his brilliant plan.

"Ethan, you need to leave," Nova blurted out awkwardly.

"Ouch."

"No, I didn't mean it like that. It's just that my dad's still up and I want to go tell him so nothing happens in the morning."

"Okay, hot girl. See you at six thirty." Ethan vaulted out the window and was out of sight quickly.

Nova tiptoed to her door and cracked it open. She could see light coming from under the office door. Tapping on it lightly, she said, "Dad? Are you in there?"

"Come in, firefly."

Nova opened the door and stepped inside. "I'm spending the day with Ethan tomorrow. He has a bunch of deliveries to do, then we're seeing a movie. Is that okay?"

Dayton frowned. "I guess so, but we need to talk about my grandmother's journal and figure out what we're doing. And we agreed to take it to Grandma Kate's to see if she could make sense of it. Don't forget you're supposed to leave for England in four days. We're running out of time."

"I know. I want to do those things. I just need this one day off. Please?"

"Sure, honey. I could use a break too, I guess. Maybe

things will be clearer if we take a step back. I don't want to wait until the last minute though."

"Neither do I. It's just one day. Then we'll make our plans."

"Okay." Dayton gave her a halfhearted smile.

"Thanks, Dad. Everything will work out. I know it."

Nova walked around the desk and hugged him before going back to her room and crawling into bed. She felt guilty for deceiving him but was determined to take matters into her own hands. If it was up to her to make things right, it was better not to involve her dad at all.

Nova's alarm went off at five thirty. She quickly showered, deciding to let her hair air dry rather than risk the blow dryer waking Alana. She was on pins and needles waiting to hear the back door slam as Celeste left for her run. At 6:20 a.m., Ethan tapped lightly on the window, once again giving her heart a lurch.

"You have to stop doing that!" Nova whispered emphatically.

"Sorry." He smiled sheepishly as he crawled inside. "Has your mom left yet?"

"No. I don't know what's taking her so long."

Nova looked at the clock again, then she crept to her bedroom door and opened it a crack just in time to see Celeste coming out of her room. Nova stepped back quickly and held her breath, praying her mom hadn't seen her. A minute later, they heard the back door close.

"Thank God. She almost saw me!" Nova shivered.

"Should we wait a minute, then go out the back?" he whispered.

"Where's your truck?"

"Parked at the bus stop."

"I hope my mom doesn't notice it! I can see her now, storming back in here and accusing you of spending the night!" Nova giggled nervously.

"Yeah, that would suck. Does your dad really have a shotgun?" Ethan actually seemed worried.

"Not that I know of. But I'm not sure. I don't think he'd shoot you though." Nova laughed out loud, then clamped her hand over her mouth and froze. There was no sound in the house. Relieved, she grabbed her backpack and headed to the window. "We'd better get out of here before one of us blows it."

"Really? We're going out the window?"

"Yes. I don't want to take any chances. We're leaving the way you came in. Wait…" Nova ran lightly around the bed, pulled the coin from Aunt Jean's out of the nightstand drawer and dropped it in her pocket.

"What's that?" Ethan asked.

"A pirate coin."

"Where'd you get that?"

"Aunt Jean's."

"Was she…? Never mind."

Nova threw her bag on the ground and climbed out with Ethan right behind her. After closing the window, they scooted around the side of the house and across the backyard to his truck. Nova pulled the map out of her bag as he pulled away.

"Next stop, Frederick, New Hampshire." Ethan smiled. "I hope you know how to get there because I still get lost around town."

"Trust me." Nova smiled.

"God help us," he said.

They drove across the bridge, turned right through town, and took I-84E toward Hartford.

"So far, so good," Ethan remarked after a while. He sounded a little on edge. Apparently, he was genuinely worried about driving so far.

"It'll be fine. It's not that complicated. I'm following my dad's route. See?" She held it up. "He drew it in marker."

Ethan kept his eyes on the road, refusing to look at the map. "Tell me where to go and don't make me look at the map while I'm driving."

Nova grinned. "You're so cute."

"Why do I feel like I've just been insulted?" He laughed.

"Just relax and drive," Nova said, giving his arm a tap with her elbow.

They were on I-84E for what seemed like a very long time. Nova kept watching for the Massachusetts Turnpike, but when they finally came to it, she almost missed it.

"Oh my gosh! Take this exit!" she yelled.

Ethan jerked the wheel a little too hard to the right, and they almost ran off the road. "Are you trying to kill us? I thought you knew where you were going!"

"I slept most of the way up with my dad. I'll be more careful. I'm really sorry I yelled at you."

"Jeez," Ethan said, nervously shaking his head

Nova managed not to miss the exit for I-495 twenty-seven miles later. For the next sixty-four miles, she filled Ethan in on everything she knew about her grandmother and how their last visit to see her had gone. Nova also told Ethan about Willow Hill, the house, the horses, and particularly Aunt Jean. She described the garden and her room with the four-poster bed and the door that led to the attic.

"I'd love to see it sometime," Ethan said hopefully.

"I'd like that too," Nova replied, imagining how wonderful it would be to have Ethan with her at Willow Hill, especially if Aunt Jean was there too.

She resolved to find a way to make that happen. If she figured out how to bring Marshall back, snagging Aunt Jean as well should be no problem. For some reason, the thought made her want to laugh, but what came out was more like a snort. Nova's face instantly turned beet red, judging by the heat radiating off of it as though she'd been in the sun for hours.

"Classy," Ethan remarked, doing his best to mimic the noise she'd just made.

Nova gave his side an impressive jab before she could catch herself. "You're hilarious," she said without any humor.

"Don't be embarrassed, hot girl. I can belch the alphabet. Want me to do it?" He grinned eagerly.

She giggled. "No, thank you."

When they were almost to Frederick, Nova nearly missed the exit again. Ethan had to avoid traffic while quickly moving over two lanes.

"Nova! If you make me wreck my truck hundreds of miles from home, my parents and yours will never let us see each other again!"

"We're not gonna wreck. And we're not *hundreds* of miles from home. It's not even two hundred."

"Whatever. Just do your navigating thing and don't kill us."

"Fine. Ethan," she said as if she were talking to a five-year-old, "drive down this road until you pass a bandstand. That's a thing that looks like a round porch without a house attached to it."

"This is an interesting side of you," Ethan said dryly.

"Just doing my navigating thing," she said sweetly in her best Southern accent.

"Hey look at that!" Ethan pointed at the ODD FELLOWS HALL sign perched atop the building on their left.

"Yeah. Apparently my family had something to do with that." Nova laughed.

"I believe it. Your family is kind of odd. You know, with the whole time travel thing."

Nova goosed him in the side again. "You're funny."

"Don't mess with the driver, young lady," he cautioned halfheartedly. "Really, though, what does it mean? Odd Fellows."

"I can't remember exactly what Dad said about them, but the original group started in England. They came here in the early 1800s, and one of my ancestors helped establish it. His name was William Grant."

"That's pretty cool."

"Yeah, I guess it is." She smiled. Her family was

pretty amazing.

Shortly after passing through the main part of town, they turned onto Harvard Street and followed it to the end, almost missing Grandma Kate's driveway again.

"She should cut some of this back," Ethan said as he tried to steer his truck around some of the debris. When the house came into sight, he whistled. "Okay, I was not expecting this. It's really nice. She has as much landscaping as we do."

"I know. I couldn't believe it when Dad and I came here before. It's so much prettier than you think it's gonna be when you see that ratty driveway."

"What did your grandmother say when you told her we were coming?" Ethan asked as he pulled up in front of the house.

Nova's mouth dropped open. "Oh my God, I didn't tell her. In all the excitement, I forgot. She's not expecting us."

Ethan stared at her in horror. "She didn't know you were coming? And bringing your boyfriend? And talking to her about traveling?"

"When you put it like that, it sounds pretty bad."

Nova's voice sounded strange because her throat had gone bone-dry. "I can't believe I did this."

"Well, you did. So what now? We can't just sit in the truck until she notices us."

"No. I guess not." Nova hesitated, then opened the door and got out.

Ethan followed her up the steps to the front door.

The blinds moved in one of the front windows, so Nova called, "Grandma Kate! It's me, Nova!"

They stood there waiting for her to open the door, but nothing happened. Nova knocked several times and called out again, but she still didn't open the door.

"Maybe she's not home," Ethan offered.

"I saw the blinds move. She's in there." Nova was getting frustrated, so she tried the door handle. Locked.

"Grandma Kate, it's just me, Nova. And Ethan. He's my boyfriend."

They heard the latch click before the door slowly opened a little. "Nova?"

"Yes, Grandma, it's me."

At that, Kate threw open the door. "Good heavens! I wasn't expecting you!"

"I know. I'm so sorry I forgot to call first." Nova motioned toward Ethan. "This is my boyfriend, Ethan."

Kate studied him for a minute then must have decided he was harmless because she opened the door wide and told them to come in. "I'm so happy to see you, Nova! After you and your dad came, I thought... well, I wasn't sure you'd come back. But here you are."

"I'm glad to see you too," Nova replied sincerely. "Dad and I felt really awful leaving things the way we did."

"Well, that's water under the bridge now." Kate smiled warmly. "You must be hungry. I just made a pot of vegetable beef soup if you'd like some."

"That sounds great!" Ethan spoke up.

"So he does talk!" Kate laughed and her eyes sparkled.

For that moment, Nova could imagine the girl Aunt Jean had described. There was definitely more to Kate than they'd given her credit for. Maybe she'd help them after all.

Kate pulled out three bowls and spooned in the thick soup. "You must think that's all I cook, Nova, but I love it. There's never a time that I don't have some fresh soup in this house. I grow the vegetables right out back in my garden. Maybe you kids would like to see it."

"Sure," Nova and Ethan said almost in unison.

While they ate, Kate told them all about her vegetable garden. She obviously spent a lot of time working in it. Nova figured that, living here by herself, that was all she had to do.

"Finish your soup and we'll go out there," she said eagerly. "You kids can take some beans and tomatoes home to your parents."

"I'm sure they'd like that." Nova looked at Ethan and he gave her a "get to it" look. She tried to figure out how to bring up why they'd come, but Grandma Kate did it for her.

"I can't believe your parents let you drive here alone." She shook her head. "Did you come all this way just to see me?"

Nova cleared her throat. "Yes. We wanted to talk to you, to ask you about Evelyn's journal."

Kate's whole demeanor changed. "Now why would you want to do that?"

Nova pulled the journal out of her bag. "There are some things I don't understand."

Kate's eyes darted to Ethan, then back to Nova. "Don't you think this should be a private conversation?"

"Oh." Nova cleared her throat. "It's okay. He knows."

"Is he a…"

"No, Grandma. He's not a traveler."

Kate stared at her incredulously. "You told him?"

"Yes. It's a long story." Nova was anxious to get down to business as minutes were ticking by and they

couldn't be late getting home. She decided to dive right in. "In your mother's journal, she talks about using someone else's timeline to change yours. When I was here with Dad, you remembered Marshall. It was like you were in more than one timeline. This one, but also the one where he exists. If that's true, can you bring him back?"

Kate's eyes lost their sparkle, and her voice sounded weary, defeated. "It's not like that. It's true that timelines can become… blurred. But it's more of a memory issue than a reality issue. I just got confused. I'm not in any other timelines, only this one. And in this one, Marshall is like my Danny. Just a memory."

"Then what does she mean about using another traveler's timeline?"

"I don't know for sure what she meant. But I think you can use someone else's timeline if all of the people involved are there, living at the same time. But you can't use it to bring back someone who never existed. You could possibly go back far enough to influence events through someone else and maybe that would make a difference, but I've never heard of anyone attempting it. My mother was quite the innovative thinker, always coming up with ideas on how we could use the gift more effectively. I'm not like her." Grandma Kate sighed. "I'm afraid you've come to the wrong person."

"There isn't anyone else to come to," Nova said angrily, shocking everyone at the table. She lowered her voice. "I'm sorry. I just can't believe there's nothing you can do! Look what she says here. 'There are powers that haven't been realized.' What does she mean? You must have heard her talk about it over the years. You lived in the same house."

"It's best to leave some things alone. You have no idea the damage you could cause."

"I'd be careful. I swear." Nova laid her hand on her grandmother's.

"Nova, even if there was something else, another way… I couldn't help you. It's been too long."

"Then tell me! What other way? Let me take the risk. All you have to do is explain how to do it."

"I heard my mother talk about a lot of things, mostly crazy ideas. I don't remember what they were, and there's no point trying."

"You mean you won't try to remember even for your grandson? When you lost Danny, Evelyn was still alive. Why didn't you ask her then? Maybe she could have helped you!"

"Don't you think I know that? I've known for years that my mother may have been able to get my family back. It seemed like she could do anything. My mother knew things she never told us because she thought they were too dangerous. If my head had been right, I would have asked her to use her knowledge to help. But at the time, I was so bitter I didn't want anyone around me. I realized years later how wrong I'd been, but by then it was too late. I couldn't change a thing. Even though I lost Daniel when I was young, he was still alive somewhere, probably having a normal life with another family. Would it have been right for me to break that up? Even if I didn't care about them, I still couldn't do anything about it. Because if I did, it would mean that you, your dad, everyone that came from my marriage to Sheldon would be gone. I decided a very long time ago that as devastating as it was to lose my little Danny, it was better to leave it alone."

"But now we've lost Marshall too, and you *can* do something about that. I know there must be a way that we can all be together, all of us alive in the same timeline. Can you go back? Visit your mother and ask her what to do?"

"I can't. I don't have the ability anymore. Don't think it's because I don't know how you feel. I understand exactly how you feel. It's hard to breathe from the weight of the grief and guilt. But trust me, the more you meddle with it, the worse it gets."

"Grandma, I'm planning to do something, with or without you," Nova said solemnly.

"I can't stop you. Do what you think you have to. But trust me when I say you don't want my help. Everything I touch dies or goes wrong. I'm not like my sister... or my mother."

Kate turned and walked up the stairs. If she had looked back, she would have seen Nova staring at her, tears running down her face. A moment later, they heard a door close upstairs.

Nova turned to Ethan. "This is exactly what happened last time. Why did I think it was a good idea to come back here?"

Ethan put his arms around her. "You were right. She's hiding something because she scared. Go up and talk to her one more time."

"It's pointless." Nova sobbed, laying her head against his chest.

"Then let me go."

Nova looked up at Ethan, and his face was dead

serious. "Okay. Go. It's the room beside the stairs to the third floor." She reached into her pocket and extracted the coin. "Give her this."

"Why?"

"It was in the attic at Willow Hill. Maybe if she has something from there…"

Ethan took the coin from her, turned and walked up the stairs. At the top, he looked back and she motioned for him to go right. He winked before disappearing down the upstairs hallway.

Nova sat in a rocker on the porch for almost thirty minutes. When Ethan appeared, she jumped up.

"What happened?" she asked breathlessly.

"Go say goodbye to her. Then I'll tell you." Ethan smiled.

Nova ran inside. Kate was packing them some cookies for the trip home.

"Grandma! Uh… did you and Ethan have a nice talk?" Nova asked nervously.

"Yes, we did. That's a nice young man you have there. I'm sorry I went upstairs. That's the way I am, I'm afraid. My sister used to tell me I avoided confrontation. I guess she's right. But I'm glad you came to see me. Promise me you'll come back when things settle down." Kate looked hopeful.

"I will," Nova replied, throwing her arms around her fragile grandmother. "I promise."

"That's good. Now take these cookies. I know young people can't go ten minutes without eating something." She laughed, following Nova out to the porch. "Give your mom and dad my love!"

"I will," Nova replied.

When she and Ethan pulled away, Kate was still on the porch, waving.

Nova could hardly contain herself. "I have to know *now*. What did she say to you?"

"Not much about traveling." Ethan laughed. "But she

told me about your dad when he was a kid and how he started writing as soon as he could hold a pencil. Apparently keeping journals is a big thing in your family. They start young. Then she went into this long thing about *The Wizard of Oz*."

"Seriously?" Nova asked, disappointed. "That's what you two talked about? *The Wizard of Oz*?"

"Yeah. But it was like she was trying to hint at something, because she wanted to make sure I told you the story."

"So tell me."

"Well… wait. How do I get back to the road we came in on?"

"Just keep going through town. I'll show you when we get to the exit," Nova said impatiently.

"Okay, apparently your dad watched the movie once when he was a kid and never would again, even though it came on every year. There was something he hated about the ending. Something that upset him."

"What was it?" Nova was confused. What did the movie have to do with anything?

"You're gonna hate this." Ethan chuckled. "She said for you to ask your dad."

"Well, that sucks. I thought she told you something important and that's why she was so happy when we left."

"She was happy because I told her you understood how she felt and wouldn't ask her about traveling anymore. I told her she didn't need to do anything, just be your grandmother."

"You told her that?" Nova suddenly felt ashamed by how she'd acted with Kate. It wasn't fair to expect her to repair damage she didn't cause. "Thanks, Ethan. That was really nice."

"No problem. Oh, and she liked the coin. When I gave it to her, she got all excited and said she remembered when she and *Jeannie* used to play with the pirate coins when they were little at 'the old house.' That's when she said to ask your dad about the Wizard of Oz."

“I still don’t get it.”

“Just ask him. But right now, you need to tell me how to get us home. If it’s up to me we’ll end up in Canada.”

CHAPTER 23

When they pulled into Nova's driveway three hours later, Celeste was out of the door before Ethan turned off the truck.

"Nova Grant! Where have you been?" she demanded. "We've been worried sick! We called everyone we know to ask if they'd seen you. Ethan's parents are worried too!"

"I'm sorry. We, uh, t-took a road trip. We didn't think it was a big deal," Nova said.

"Not a big deal? You lied to us about where you were going! Ethan lied to his parents too. You better give me some answers, young lady!" She turned to Ethan, who backed up as though he thought she was going to hit him. "Ethan, go home!"

He hesitated for a second, then hopped back in his truck, backed out of the driveway, and drove away. Nova watched him disappear around the corner as an overpowering sense of dread washed over her. She turned back to Celeste and opened her mouth to say something, but her mother cut her off.

"Get in the house!" Celeste turned and stormed in ahead of her.

Dayton was standing in the foyer, fuming. "Was this Ethan's idea? To lie to your parents and take off to God knows where?"

Nova's heart was racing. In all her planning, she hadn't even thought about this scenario, so she had no backup story. She'd just have to take whatever punishment her parents dished out.

"Do you have any idea how worried I've been?" Celeste broke down sobbing and threw her arms around Nova. "I didn't know what to think. We don't even know this boy!"

"I didn't mean to worry you." Nova hugged her mother and decided that she'd just tell the truth. "We went to Grandma Kate's. I felt like seeing her and wanted her to meet Ethan. I didn't think you and Dad would let us go, so I lied. It was wrong, and I'm really sorry."

Dayton was obviously taken aback. "You went to see your grandmother? In Frederick?"

"Yes. She made us lunch and sent us home with cookies." Nova realized she'd left them in the truck. "Okay, she sent Ethan home with cookies."

"Why didn't you say you wanted to go see Kate?" Celeste asked, a little calmer. "We could have all gone this weekend."

"I'm sorry." Nova couldn't think of anything else to say.

"What you did was reckless," Dayton said, frowning. "Something could have happened to you and we'd have had no idea where you were."

Celeste found her resolve again. "You're grounded. And no Ethan for a month after we get back from Europe!"

"A month?" Nova asked incredulously. "That's not fair!"

"Just go to your room." Dayton pointed down the hallway.

Nova trudged down the hall, utterly dejected. A whole month without Ethan. Actually two months if you counted the time she was supposed to be in Europe. She closed her door and dropped her bag on the floor, wondering where Alana was. She'd been conspicuously absent during the whole tirade. Nova wanted to see her but wasn't anxious to leave her room, so she sat on her bed. Other than getting to spend the entire day with Ethan, the trip had been a bust. And now she was grounded. She could travel back to yesterday and not go to Grandma Kate's, but then her sister and her dad would know they were repeating time and she'd have that to deal with.

Dayton tapped on her door and opened it without waiting for a response. Once inside, he pulled the door closed and studied her a moment before speaking. "You were hoping to travel today, weren't you?"

"No, not travel. I wanted to ask her about the journal, what Evelyn meant when she said you could use someone else's timeline. And the other part about having more possibilities. I thought if I went back with her mother's journal, she'd talk to me."

"And did she?" he asked soberly.

"Not really." Nova shook her head. "She said basically the same thing she said before. It was a waste of time."

Dayton sat in her blue armchair. He looked as though he'd aged ten years in one day. Where was her boyish dad? *Chalk that up to another thing I've lost.*

"Maybe I need to go back there alone," he mumbled.

Nova remembered what Grandma Kate had said to Ethan. For some reason, she'd wanted Nova to ask her dad about the movie. "Dad, do you remember *The Wizard of Oz*?"

Dayton looked up. "What?"

"*The Wizard of Oz*. You know, the movie."

"Of course I know the movie. What about it?"

"Grandma Kate told Ethan you hated it when you were little. There was something about the ending that bothered you, and after that first time, you never watched it again. She said I should ask you what you didn't like about it."

Dayton stared at her. "*The Wizard of Oz*? That's what she wanted to talk about?"

"Yes. What didn't you like about the ending?" Nova

pressed.

Dayton frowned at first. Then he smiled slightly. "I hated the fact that she went through all the barriers—the witch, the flying monkeys, the poppies—when she could have gone home the whole time."

Neither of them spoke for a couple of minutes, then Nova smiled. "Are you thinking what I'm thinking?"

"Yes, I am." Dayton's eyes lit up. "She was trying to tell us something. I'm going back to Frederick. And you're coming too."

"I'm grounded," Nova pointed out.

"I'll work it out with your mom," Dayton promised, still smiling. "Get some rest, firefly. We'll talk in the morning."

He kissed her forehead before leaving the room and shutting the door. Nova walked over quietly and flipped the lock. She didn't want anyone else walking in. All she wanted to do was sleep.

Nova felt as though her head was swimming. Why hadn't Grandma Kate just said whatever it was she was hinting at? It was so frustrating. Nova hopped off the bed and grabbed boxers and a T-shirt from her dresser. For a moment, she was tempted to click her heels together… just in case.

She changed quickly and crawled into bed, exhausted. Just as her head hit the pillow, her window flew open.

Nova jumped up again, her heart pounding. "Ethan! What are you doing here! I can't believe your parents let you out of the house!"

"Keep it down! I don't want *your* parents coming in here," he whispered as he climbed in the window. "I didn't think your dad was ever gonna leave."

"Did you see me change clothes?" she asked, embarrassed.

"Nah." He winked, grinning.

"I thought you went home."

"I did. They sent me to my room—grounded. I'm still in there as far as they know."

"You should go back. I don't want you getting into more trouble because of me."

"No way, hot girl. I had to make sure you were okay." He came over and put his arms around her.

"I'm fine. Just freaked a little from my mom's meltdown in the front yard."

"Yeah? Well, you should have been at my house. Talk about meltdown."

"What are we gonna do? My mom said I can't see you for two months."

"We'll figure out a way, hot girl. I promise. I'll come up with an apology that'll satisfy her." He looked at her and winked.

"I believe you." Nova smiled up at him before laying her head against his chest. "I'm so tired. I need to go to sleep." Nova pulled away. "Go home. I'll talk to you tomorrow, okay?"

Ethan stood there for a minute, then he walked over to her bed and piled the pillows against the headboard.

"What are you doing?"

"I just want to stay here for a while if that's all right with you. No expectations. I promise." Ethan sat on her bed, his back against the pillows, and patted the spot beside him. "Just a little while longer. I don't know how hard it's gonna be to get out of the house again."

Nova climbed up beside him and laid her head on his shoulder. "Ethan, why are you being so great to me?"

"I love you, hot girl."

"But why are you okay with me wanting to change everything to get my brother back? Last time... well, you didn't take it this well. You said you didn't want to lose me."

"I'm not gonna lose you. I'll be there in every timeline. You said so yourself."

"But what if next time is different? What if I try to talk to you about all of this and you think I've lost it. That's what you thought this time until I told you about the bracelet. What if there isn't a bracelet next time? I want to be able to talk to you about traveling, even if I'm happy with the way things work out. It's amazing to be able to share it. I'd hate to have to keep it a secret from you."

Ethan thought for a moment, then he pulled her up into a sitting position facing him. "When I was in the second grade, we lived over near Stamford. There were these two guys from Sam's class who lived down the street. For some reason, they loved to torment me when Sam wasn't around. One day they locked me in their basement all afternoon. They told me there were ghosts down there, and the whole time I was locked in, they ran around outside, making noises to scare me. When they finally let me out, they told me not to tell anyone or they'd leave me down there next time and no one would ever find me. My parents were freaked out with me gone all afternoon. They called the cops and everything."

"Oh my God, that's awful! What happened to those boys?"

"Nothing. I never told anyone, not even Sam. I knew if I told him, he'd get in a fight with them and either get hurt or in trouble. The next summer, we moved here and I never saw those guys again. No one else knows about it. If I don't believe you next time, just tell me you know about the time Riley and Josh locked me in their basement. Trust me. That'll do it."

"Riley and Josh. Got it." She smiled, thinking about meeting Ethan all over again in a perfect timeline where everyone she loved was alive. *There has to be a way.*

CHAPTER 24

Nova closed her eyes and was nearly asleep when her mind kicked back on, repeating something Aunt Jean had told her when she traveled back to the summer of her fifteenth birthday at Willow Hill. She sat bolt upright, wide awake.

"Ethan, something is bothering me. Aunt Jean seemed certain that my great-grandmother's journal would tell me a way to get Marshall back. She was right about everything else. How could she be wrong about that?"

Ethan frowned. "Maybe she wasn't wrong. You just haven't figured it out yet."

Nova climbed off the bed and retrieved Evelyn's journal from her backpack. "Most of what's in here is basically what Aunt Jean told me at Willow Hill. Other than Evelyn's own personal experiences with traveling, it's just telling me things I already know. That is… until you get to the end."

Ethan sat up and took the journal, scanning the entries until he came to the last page. "What does this last entry mean?"

Nova took the journal back and read it again.

"There are some things I hesitate to share, as they may only cause the others to take unnecessary risks. And yet, I wonder. The Grants who came before often married within the family name. Their children possessed stronger abilities

and weren't confined to some of the normal limitations. Still, this knowledge is a burden I hesitate to pass on. Perhaps it would be better to keep the rules as they are."

"I've racked my brain, but I don't know what it means. It's one of the things I'd hoped Grandma Kate would know. Evelyn was a Grant by birth. She married her second cousin, who was also a Grant, so she's obviously talking about her own descendants."

"Like you," Ethan pointed out.

"I guess so. But what special abilities could I have? Why didn't she just come out and say it?"

"Okay, what are the rules you know about when it comes to traveling?"

"You can only travel back and forth in your own timeline, and other travelers can feel it if they're close by."

"That's it?"

"No. There are other rules, like being able to jump back for a visit and return to where you started as long as you don't stay too long."

"Explain?"

"I'm not in the mood. I need to think—"

"But your great-grandmother talks about breaking the rules. What would be the one rule you'd break if you could?"

Nova mulled over that question for a few minutes. In her limited experience, she had only caused one timeline switch. *If I could change one rule, what would it be?* Nova knew the answer before she'd finished asking herself the question. *I'd want the connection from when I traveled to still be there, so I could go back to that night at Aunt Jean's, the night I brought Alana back. I'd want a chance to try again.* A chill ran up her spine as she stared at the page again.

"And yet, there are powers that haven't been realized, and shouldn't those powers be explored? This gift of traveling is both complicated and awe-inspiring. Every time we travel, it leaves a thread behind, and that thread is woven

into an elaborate and beautiful tapestry made up of all the times we've traveled, combined with those of travelers around us who have moved in and out of our lives. If others could see this tapestry, they would be amazed and humbled by its complexity and beauty. What would the possibilities be if we weren't confined by rules? Maybe, when time runs out, we will finally know, and regret the loss of what could have been."

The corner of the page was turned down. When Nova lifted the flap, her breath caught in her throat. *"The tapestry is the key,"* was written under the flap.

Nova stared at the note, and slowly a light went off in her head. "Oh my God. This note on the side... the handwriting isn't the same." She threw her arms around Ethan and hugged him tightly. "Ethan! This is it! What Aunt Jean was talking about! This is her handwriting! She must have written this after I traveled back to see her at Willow Hill the second time! She said she'd do what she could. She knew I'd find the journal a year later. She wrote that note to me!"

"Okay, so what does she mean? What's the key?"

"Evelyn says that every time you travel, it leaves a thread. That's how you can get back to where you started. That's why Grandma Kate wanted me to ask Dad about *The Wizard of Oz*! I'm Dorothy!"

"What?"

"That's what Grandma Kate was trying to tell us! We've gone all over the place, trying to find help to get back to where we started, when Marshall was alive. But it's all been pointless. One dead end after another. I think she's telling me I can do it myself! That I could have all along! The threads are still there even if I can't feel them!"

"But I thought you only had a short time before it was too late to go back," Ethan said. "You said you lost the connection."

"Yes! That's what Aunt Jean said, but *her* mother

says the connection is still there! That's what the threads are. I'm strong, like Evelyn. Aunt Jean said so herself. I need to find the thread that will take me back to the moment I traveled at Willow Hill. And to do that, I need to find the tapestry!"

"Okay… how?" Ethan was uncertain. "Didn't you already try?"

"I looked for a thread, not a tapestry. I was looking for one connection. Somehow, I need to find what Evelyn was talking about. She's seen it. I know she has. The line back to that night is there, along with every other time I've traveled. I just need to find the right one."

"So let me get this straight. You traveled and brought Alana back while you were at your aunt's house, right?"

"Right."

"And now you want to go back to that moment, before Alana came back, because…?"

"Because that's when I lost Marshall," she said solemnly.

"If you do that, what will happen to Alana?" Ethan frowned, already knowing the answer. "She'll be dead again, right?"

"She'll be dead again."

"Nova… are you okay with that?" he asked incredulously.

"No, I'm not. It makes me sick to think about losing her again. But Marshall was innocent. What happened to Alana wasn't his fault. He shouldn't have to give up his life for hers. He didn't choose to sacrifice himself. He didn't have any say in the matter. I just did it without thinking of the consequences or what could happen to him. I *need* to bring him back. I can't live with myself if I'm the reason he isn't here. He had everything in front of him, his whole life, and I took it from him. I have to undo that. And then afterward… somehow I'm gonna get my sister back too. I'll try again. And next time I won't make the same mistakes."

"I believe you," Ethan said softly, pulling her close.

"I think you'll find a way."

"I'm praying I can, but I have to do it even if I can't." Nova felt the crushing weight of her decision. "There's something I need to do. Will you stay? Wait for me?"

"Always, hot girl." He kissed her gently on the cheek.

Nova jumped out of bed and tiptoed into the hall before quietly opening her sister's door. Alana was sleeping, curled up with the covers wrapped around her, a butterfly still in its cocoon. Her hair swirled around her face, hiding all but her mouth. How many times had Nova studied the sketches of her sister, always noticing the way her mouth curved up slightly at the edges? And now she was here, alive and well. Having her back had been the most wonderful thing to ever happen, even if it was only for a short while. Nova desperately hoped that they'd be together again after tonight, after she did the terrible thing she had to do.

Alana continued to sleep, blissfully unaware of what Nova was planning. Nova stood perfectly still, studying every detail so she wouldn't forget. A strand of hair fell over her sister's mouth and fluttered as she breathed in and out. Nova moved it away.

Alana opened her eyes, only half awake. "What are you doing, little sister?"

"I just wanted to say good night," Nova answered softly, hoping Alana couldn't tell she was crying.

"You're in so much trouble. I'm actually a little jealous. Crazy stunts are usually my thing, not yours," she muttered.

"I know. It was good though."

"Go to bed. We can hang out tomorrow since Ethan's off-limits." Alana was falling back to sleep. "I'll see you in the morning."

"I'll see you," Nova said softly.

"Night, little sister…" Smiling, Alana turned over and pulled the covers around her again. Almost immediately, her breathing became regular.

"Good night, Allie." Nova stood there with tears

running down her face, watching her sister drift off. "I'm so sorry," she whispered. "I promise I'll come back to get you."

Nova crept out of the room and gently closed the door. Sitting on her bed beside Ethan, she allowed herself a few more minutes before finally leaning back against the pillows.

"When are you gonna do it?" he asked.

"Now, I guess. Maybe you should leave." Nova felt as though she'd been up for days. The emotional strain had worn her down and she wasn't sure she had the strength to do anything, much less travel in time.

"I want to stay… if it won't make it impossible for you to, uh, do it. I mean, you were able to at my house so…"

"That was different. This is something completely new. I need to be able to concentrate."

"I know. I just want to be with you as long as I can." He pulled her close and kissed her.

"Stay then. But you have to let me focus."

"All right, hot girl."

"Ethan, you know you won't be here when it's done."

"I know."

"I might not even be able to find it—the connection."

Ethan kissed her again, then moved away slightly. "You'll find it. I love you."

"I love you too."

Nova laid her head back against the pillows and closed her eyes, willing herself to relax. Ethan took her hand. After several minutes, she felt the tension leaving her body. Keeping her breathing regular, she tried to block out everything else. It always helped if she could latch onto a sound from far away. There were crickets outside her window, but her mind refused to connect to their chirping.

She continued to breathe rhythmically and let her brain focus where it would. Ethan had apparently drifted off because his hand had gone limp in hers and his breathing had changed. The thought that he may be a traveler too crossed her mind again, but she shook it off. She listened to him breathing steadily. Blocking out everything else, she focused on the sound he made as he took each breath.

Minutes passed before she felt anything, but then it began as it always did—with the sensation of floating. She felt her body becoming lighter and lighter, waiting for a destination. She searched with her mind. It had to be there somewhere.

Refusing to allow herself to hone in on a target in time, she searched instead for the tapestry her great-grandmother had described. It had to be real. Evelyn must have seen it. Otherwise, how would she have known? And somewhere in that tapestry was the thread that would take her back to Willow Hill, back to the night that had cost Marshall his life.

She continued to feel herself floating, still with no direction. *Where is it?* Her brain wanted to take her somewhere, anywhere, flooding her with visions of her life and the people in it. She shook them off, keeping her mind as clear as possible. *It's there. I know it is...*

Nova let her mind wander around, searching. Her head began to hurt. A little at first, then the pounding started, relentlessly with each heartbeat. The visions became more intense, each one flashing brilliantly before her. Nova put her hands over her eyes, trying to block them out. It was no use. Her eyes were already closed. The visions were in her head.

Her body was being jerked around, as if submerged in a churning river. Not the river that Aunt Jean had described. This one was violent—a raging body of water yanking her in every direction, trying to smash her against the rocks. The visions kept coming—every event in this life and others, bombarding her with information, straining her senses to the breaking point. Everything and everyone was there—

Marshall, her parents, Ethan, Willow Hill, Aunt Jean, her house, the bridge, all of the people and places she'd known. Soon, she feared, her overloaded brain would explode from the assault. She had to stop it somehow. Nova steeled herself against the current and focused on the visions, forcing them back with every ounce of will she possessed. Almost instantly, it all stopped.

There was nothing around her now. The images had vanished and she could no longer hear Ethan breathing rhythmically beside her. Now she seemed to be in a dark tunnel void of any connections to the past or future. Alarmed, she strained to see something in the darkness, some glimpse of a memory. Where had they all gone? It was as if she had no past and no future. Nothing. What if she were stuck here, floating in this void for eternity?

Nova fought the panic welling up. She continued to search the darkness frantically, but to no avail. Maybe she was still on the bed next to Ethan and this blackness was an illusion, a trick of the mind. Nova listened, trying to hear him breathing. But there was no sound. She desperately tried to connect with something, anything. But there was nothing there, just emptiness.

As she continued to float, her headache subsided until all that remained was an odd sensation of pressure in her temples. Slowly, a sense of peace covered her like a warm blanket. The darkness didn't seem as forbidding now. She had an undeniable feeling of expectation, as if she were about to discover something amazing. It was just ahead, on the other side of a curtain that was blotting out any trace of light. All she had to do was pull it away. On the other side would be what she was looking for.

She floated along in the darkness, waiting anxiously to break through, for something to appear. And then the curtain dissolved and there it was—a faint glimmer, seemingly far away, of what looked like a silver cloud. Nova strained to see, unable to make out a form. It seemed to go off in every direction, gradually becoming thinner until it disappeared entirely into the void.

Nova found that she could float toward it at will. She wasn't sure how she was powering her movement, because it just happened. Maybe she'd been moving forward all along and hadn't realized it in the darkness. As she neared the strange cloud, she saw that it was made up of hundreds of silvery strands, more like an elaborate and dense spider web than a tapestry. Now utterly calm, she knew instinctively that this web was formed not just by her timelines, but others as well. There were threads that signified other lives that had little or nothing to do with hers, but had intersected and influenced hers at some point. How many times had she passed through someone else's life, unaware of the effect she'd had on them as well, however minute?

Nova floated effortlessly into the interior of the web, the thread of each timeline weaving all around her on every side. From this vantage point, she could see how vast and deep it was. The threads that had all seemed to be the same shimmering silver actually glowed with subtly different hues. She was drawn to the ones that radiated a particular shade of blue and knew instinctively that they were hers. It was difficult to see where they came from or where they led. Each time one of her threads intersected with another, hers shot off from that point in both directions. Other travelers had changed their timelines in subtle ways that had affected hers. It seemed to have happened countless times. Tiny changes that had gone unnoticed.

Nova touched one of her glowing blue strands and was instantly jolted by a vivid image of herself at that exact moment. She was somewhere in England with her dad, walking through what appeared to be a museum. She heard the docent describing the various objects around them. He had taken her on one of his trips, just as he'd promised he would!

Exhilarated, she touched another strand and another image flashed before her. She was four or five years old, in the pasture at Willow Hill, picking flowers with Aunt Jean while a mare and foal grazed near them. Nova was infatuated with the ability she seemed to now possess—the ability to visit any time in any reality, past, present, and future. It was captivating.

She carefully touched each strand, marveling at how

easy it was becoming. There was no headache now. No sensation of being pulled around. She felt powerful, in control, touching each timeline with her mind and seeing events both past and future in each one. She was able to take in a moment as it happened or fly through as if she'd pushed a fast forward button.

Rocketing through one image after another, she discovered that some of them were remarkably similar, almost as if she were seeing the same reality that existed in another thread. If she followed it along, she eventually came to an event that occurred only in that life—an event that changed the direction of that particular timeline. She found herself engrossed in each journey, fascinated by the subtle changes that caused a specific thread to shoot off in another direction. She continued to visit strand after strand, watching herself move through different realities. She had no idea how long she'd been inside the tapestry, and she didn't care. She wanted to stay there, browsing through timelines as if watching an endless movie that included decades of deleted scenes.

And then suddenly, there it was. She saw the rental car turning in through the stone entrance at Willow Hill for the first time. She watched it move slowly up the long driveway to the house. Aunt Jean stood on the porch in her yellow shirt and riding boots. The horses in the pasture that bordered the drive barely reacted to the strange car passing by—all except for a colt frolicking around his mother as she grazed contentedly. He kicked up his heels and raced along the fence, just behind the car. Nova hadn't noticed him when they'd arrived before because she'd been fixated on the house and Aunt Jean.

Anxious to reach the night she'd traveled, Nova moved forward on the timeline and saw herself in the attic, discovering the painting of Grandma Kate with her first family. Each time she paused on a scene, she felt a tug, as if the timeline was trying to pull her in. As she watched herself in the attic, she felt it. The longer she stayed in that spot, the more it tried to draw her in. All she had to do was grab that point with her mind and she'd step into that exact moment, sitting on the rough wood floor, staring at the painting of little Danny holding his toy hammer with his parents smiling at him.

Nova pulled away slightly, then cautiously touched the point just before the timeline suddenly shot off in another direction. That was it—the spot she'd been searching for. It was as if no time had passed. She was there, lying in the four-poster upstairs, listening to the clock and preparing to change all of their lives. All she had to do was go back there, step back into her life at that moment. Everything would be as it had been before. She could start over and wait until she had more control.

She hesitated, thinking about Alana. Could she really do this? How could she willingly lose her sister after all she'd gone through to get her back? But there was Marshall to think about. She couldn't sacrifice her little brother. There had to be another way. *I'll come back for you, Allie.*

Nova hesitated another moment, looking once more at the endless web of timelines surrounding her. If she stayed, maybe she'd be able to find one that included Alana and Marshall. But there were so many. Too many to count. And she may never find this one again.

She tore her eyes away from the web and touched the spot again, the connection to that night at Willow Hill, and instantly felt it pull her in like the current in a fast-flowing river. This river was strong but not as violent as the other had been. It felt safe, purposeful. She held on, throwing all of her energy at the target as she was drawn into the tunnel. This time, the sensation was pleasant. This time, she was in control. She heard the nighttime sounds of the garden, felt the smooth sheets beneath her…

Nova sat bolt upright in the four-poster, her heart pounding. The delicate scent of Aunt Jean's garden drifted in through the open window, tickling her senses. *I'm back!*

Her eyes scanned the moonlit room. Everything was

exactly as she'd left it. Her jeans and pale-pink pullover were on the chair where she'd hastily discarded them the night she traveled—or now, minutes ago. Remembering the broken seal, she glanced at the attic door, but it was closed tight. She'd have to tell Aunt Jean to fix it, because a month from now, it would probably break and the door would be stuck open, letting the demented dolls into the room. Nova laughed out loud at the thought of that conversation.

Exhilarated to be back, she tiptoed to the door, cracked it open slightly, and listened. She couldn't hear anyone upstairs, so she crept down the hall and halfway down the staircase before pausing again to listen. Her family was still on the porch, laughing and talking. She heard them through the open windows. She stole over to the window beside the swing and peered out. There Marshall was, sleeping peacefully, bits of hay sticking out of his hair. Exactly as she had envisioned.

Tears poured down Nova's cheeks. She had to use all of her strength to keep from running outside and scooping him up. That would be too hard to explain. As far as the others knew, she'd only gone upstairs a short while ago. Nova watched him for another moment, mesmerized.

"Marshall's having such a good time with the horses," Celeste's voice drifted in through the window. "It'll be a trick getting him to leave."

"It's a joy having you all here."

Nova smiled through her tears when she heard her aunt's voice. They were all here, exactly as they'd been before.

"We'd better get this guy in bed." That was Dayton. "I'll take him up."

He came over and gently lifted Marshall so as not to wake him. Anxious to avoid being seen just yet, Nova jerked away from the window, bolted up the stairs, and ran lightly down the hall to her room. After closing her door quietly, she crawled into bed and lay there a few minutes, listening to the crickets as a gentle breeze from the open window brushed across her face. She took in a deep breath and let it out slowly.

"Thank you, God," she whispered. "I'm really here."

Nova lay there another minute, listening to the faint sound of her dad carrying her little brother up the stairs and closing his door down the hall. Wiping her eyes with the back of her hand, she picked up the phone on the nightstand and punched in the number.

He answered on the first ring, sounding wide-awake, as if he'd been waiting for her. "What's up, hot girl?"

Nova smiled. "Ethan, I have so much to tell you."

THE END